"I can make you come right now,"
Hank told her. *"Just say yes."*

Oh, God, how Sam wanted to. She pushed her aching nipple farther into his palm and whimpered when he thumbed it through her shirt.

"I'll take you to the edge, as many times as you want, I promise." He licked her neck, creating a blaze of sensation. "Starting right now. All you have to do is tell me..."

Hank found her mouth and kissed her deeply. His hand left her breast and slowly moved lower, slipping beneath her waistband, then beneath her panties. At the first brush of those talented fingers, a startled cry broke from her lips.

His hot breath fanned against her ear. "All you have to do is say yes..." he whispered.

A shiver shook her. *Ahhh,* this felt good, Sam thought. But the warm tingling feeling had only just started when Hank moved his hand, making her inhale sharply, bringing her instantly to the peak.

"Yes, yes, *yes!*" Sam cried, reveling in the waves of exquisite sensation as her first ever orgasm ripped through her.

Dear Reader,

When the idea behind this book first came to me, it really struck a chord. I think at some point in our lives we all go through an ugly-duckling stage—and some of us stay in it longer than others! Let's face it, the things we go through during those awkward years are enough to make any woman question her self-worth. After all, we live in a world where the words *thin* and *perfect* are synonymous with beauty.

But it isn't right. And so, in *The Sex Diet,* I'm taking authorial license to write about things the way they *should* be. My heroine, Samantha McCafferty, is the ultimate ugly duckling. Only, she's not going to take it lying down...at least, not yet. First, she has a plan. She's going to do whatever it takes to have Hank Masterson, her first and only love, right where she wants him—in her bed! And if she's lucky, she might even be able to keep him there.

I hope you enjoy Hank and Samantha's story. And for those of you thinking about trying the sex diet themselves, watch out for allergies!

Happy reading!

Rhonda Nelson

P.S. Be sure to visit me at my Web site, www.BooksByRhondaNelson.com.

Books by Rhonda Nelson

THE SEX DIET
Rhonda Nelson

HARLEQUIN®

TORONTO • NEW YORK • LONDON
AMSTERDAM • PARIS • SYDNEY • HAMBURG
STOCKHOLM • ATHENS • TOKYO • MILAN • MADRID
PRAGUE • WARSAW • BUDAPEST • AUCKLAND

This book is dedicated to a wonderful woman whom I love
and respect, a loyal friend, confidante and kindred spirit,
a cousin by relation, but a sister of the heart—
Sheila Pierce Sherrod. My life is so much richer with you in it.

ISBN 0-373-79144-5

THE SEX DIET

Copyright © 2004 by Rhonda Nelson.

This edition published by arrangement with Harlequin Books S.A.

www.eHarlequin.com

Printed in U.S.A.

1

"YOU HAVE GOT TO BE KIDDING."

The perky receptionist behind the counter of Clearwater Bed and Breakfast smiled uncomfortably. "Er...no. I don't have a reservation in your name, Ms. McCafferty."

Samantha McCafferty absently scratched her arm and squelched a vicious stab of irritation. The damned antihistamine was wearing off and if she didn't get another dose soon, she'd undoubtedly break out in ugly red hives from head to toe. That would certainly negate any appeal she might hope to garner through this sex diet, Samantha thought as she pictured her swollen, hive-covered face wearing a seductive smile. Ugh. Not pretty. She squeezed her eyes tightly shut. She didn't have time for this inconvenience. She needed that medicine *now*.

"Look, I don't care whether you've got my name in your system or not," Samantha told her, making a valiant effort to keep a note of annoyance from her tone. "I have a standing reservation. I've been vacationing here since I was a child, and have continued the tradition into my adulthood.'' She smiled sweetly. ''The first week of September, in the Oleander Suite. Put me there.'' Before I turn into one giant red blob, Sam thought, covertly scratching her side. Oh, the pains one endured to be attractive.

The receptionist—Tina, according to her name tag—winced regretfully. ''I'm afraid that room is already booked.''

''What?'' Samantha felt the first stirrings of genuine alarm and leaned forward anxiously. That couldn't possibly be right. This had to be a mistake. Her entire plan—*Operation Orgasm*—centered around this vacation. She was three days into the sex diet—the one guaranteed to make her attractive to the opposite sex—for pity's sake and, if the way the guy in seat B2 on the flight down had been acting had been any indication, it was definitely beginning to work. She couldn't afford for things to get screwed up now. Annoyed, she scratched her thigh.

''It's booked,'' Tina said apologetically and lifted her shoulders in a small shrug. ''Everything is booked. Has been since they announced the *Belle of the Beach* contest.''

Oh, no! Samantha mentally wailed. This *could not* be happening. Everything could not be booked. Surely Hank wouldn't do this to her. He couldn't have. Not this time, dammit. She'd kill him.

Samantha had been so busy pondering the everything-is-booked statement that it took a moment for the rest of what the clerk had said to filter through her turbulent thoughts, but when it did her brow furrowed. "The *Belle of the Beach* contest?" It sounded vaguely familiar, she thought. Had Hank mentioned it?

Tina gestured a manicured hand at a flyer on the wall. "Yep. It's this weekend. The winner gets an all-expense-paid trip to the Bahamas, as well as a new SUV and ten grand in prize money."

Samantha whistled low, gazed at the glitzy flyer. She could certainly use ten grand. She'd been steadily setting aside a nest egg since she'd graduated from college for a down payment on a future house, but living expenses combined with her student-loan debt had hindered her progress.

She made a good living as a dietician at one of Aspen's posh spas—Cedar Crest—but the cost of living was staggering and, for reasons she didn't fully understand, she'd recently decided it was time to return to her southern roots, move back to Orange Beach, Alabama, where she'd grown up.

Samantha had lost her parents at sixteen—victims of a drunk driver—and had moved in with her grandmother, her only living relative. Then, sadly, two years later, Gran had passed away, leaving her completely orphaned. Were it not for Hank Masterson—her longtime friend and, lamentably, the unrequited love of her life—and his parents, Samantha didn't know what she would have done. The Mastersons were her godparents and had done everything they could to help make her way easier. She'd appreciated their help, but staying in Orange Beach and attending community college just hadn't seemed right, particularly after Hank had moved away to Tuscaloosa.

Four years older than her, Hank had graduated from the University of Alabama the year she'd graduated from high school. Samantha had fully expected him to return to Orange Beach—had been particularly hurt that he hadn't—and, when he'd decided not to come home, Samantha had decided it was time for her to leave as well.

The decision had been difficult, but one that she didn't regret. She'd needed the space, the change in scenery. She'd traded sea and sand for mountains and snow and could honestly say that the move had been just the therapy she'd needed at the time. She'd moved to Colorado, attended college and made yearly pilgrimages back to Orange Beach, back to the Clearwater B&B where she'd spent so much time as a child. But over the past several years, each time she'd come home, it had grown increasingly harder to make the trip back out west.

Because Hank had returned.

He now owned the old B&B. Samantha had literally spent years of her life here in this old antebellum house snugged against the Gulf of Mexico.

She loved it here, loved the salty breezes and the squish of sand between her toes. She sighed a wistful breath, clawed at a place behind her ear. She couldn't wait to move home, but knew that until she had a substantial down payment for a house, that dream would simply have to wait. She'd take a significant cut in pay when she did make the move and she didn't want a giant mortgage hanging over her head when that time came. Unless a windfall landed in her lap, a few more years in Aspen would be in order.

Samantha smirked wryly. And that would undoubtedly be the case, she thought as she eyed the *Belle of the Beach* poster. She had about as much of a chance to win that heaving bosom, bronzed-body contest as she did to land Hank with this crazy sex diet—nil.

Like most men on the planet—with the exception of one painfully poignant moment years ago when he'd been drunk and she'd been stupid—Hank didn't seem to realize that she existed.

A sad smile drifted over her lips as she recalled that almost-kiss. She could still feel the butterflies in her belly, could still remember the frantic, desperately hopeful beat of her heart, the rush of anticipation…then the subsequent burn of humiliation when his eyes had widened and he'd stopped just short of settling his lips over hers. He'd sworn, then apologized, and Sam had pasted a brave smile on her face and pretended like the rejection hadn't hurt. But it had. Dearly.

He had no way of knowing it, of course, but that almost-kiss had been a favor in many ways. It had forced her to come to a hard truth, had forced her to realize that no matter how desperately she might want him, he would never want her. She'd resigned herself to be content with their friendship. Did she love him? Without a doubt. Would she always love him? Most definitely. But what good was love that wasn't returned? She'd turned her focus elsewhere—her career, then more recently on *Operation Orgasm* and making herself attractive.

To put it in the gentlest of terms, Samantha had been a late bloomer. She'd been a frizzy-headed, rail-thin, freckled, bespectacled wreck and she knew it.

Pictures didn't lie.

Thankfully over the past year, she'd found a good stylist and had learned how to tame her curly strawberry-blond locks, she'd gotten contacts and, by supplementing her diet with high-calorie protein milkshakes—science could put a man on the moon, but no cure yet for brain freeze?—she'd packed on twenty solid pounds in the past year. She actually had curves and had increased her bustline a full cup size, a feat she was most proud of. Sure, the contacts were a plus, and her new hairstyle was certainly flattering, but the breasts...now they were powerful. All she had to do was draw her shoulders back a little and *bam!*—self-confidence surged through her. Remarkable.

A woman had to strike while the iron was hot and luckily, she'd inadvertently stumbled upon the one thing she sincerely hoped would guarantee her success—a sex diet.

Several months ago, Samantha had accidentally found what she suspected was the perfect combination of foods to heighten sex appeal, stimulate the emission of pheromones and rejuvenate lumbering libidos. Her gaze turned inward as she remembered that bizarre day. She'd planned her menu, balanced nutritional values just like she always had. But this one week, in particular, had resulted in heightened sexual arousal in the woman and, more important, reciprocated interest in the men.

That week, trendy Cedar Crest—which prided itself on social graciousness and decorum—had all but turned into an orgy of sexual depravity that would have made the legendary parties at the Playboy mansion seem tame by comparison. The lodge had practically vibrated from the lusty sounds of sex.

Samantha had been astounded with the results and, just to make sure that it hadn't been a fluke, a month later she'd served the same menu plan to a completely new batch of clients—with the same results. She'd decided that if it could work for the Viagra set, it could certainly work for her.

It had to, because being chronically, perpetually, miserably sexually frustrated was slowly driving her mad. If she didn't have an orgasm soon, she'd undoubtedly need a little padded cell devoid of sharp objects.

But how could she not be sexually frustrated when everywhere she looked there was another reminder of her nonexistent sex life? Movies, books, commercials, television, the Internet. Hell, you couldn't thumb through a magazine without seeing a half-naked woman or a ripped guy with six-pack abs. And why? Because sex sells. And why did sex sell? Because, with the exception of very few, *everyone* wanted it, most especially herself. Young, old, rich or poor, mankind had that one thing in common—the desire, the need, the drive to procreate. Samantha's own desire had been steadily humming for a while now, but in recent months had begun to screech and wail.

She'd grown tired of reading about/watching romance and never having any for herself—it was torture. Weary of the achy feeling in her chest when she saw couples holding hands or stealing a kiss— more torture. Tired of that hollow unfulfilled sensation deep in her belly when she found herself locked in the tight jaws of unrelieved sexual frustration. Which was woefully often. She expelled a heavy breath.

In short, she was tired of never having sex, of being an OV—orgasm virgin.

But by the end of her vacation, if this diet progressed the way it should—and she had no reason to suspect that it wouldn't—*that* at least would be one less thing for her to be weary of.

Granted when the week was over she might still be alone...but at least she wouldn't be pathetic, for pity's sake. At least—provided she found a skilled lover—she would have had a real honest-to-goodness back-clawing, earth-shattering, screaming orgasm. The one and only time she'd ever had sex, it had been a miserable, awkward experience, which had lasted less than a successful bull ride. The combination of alcohol, loneliness, curiosity and screaming hormones had perpetuated the rash decision and, ultimately, she'd wasted her virginity on a bumbling, overzealous nerd who didn't know any more about the act than she did.

She wouldn't make that mistake this time—this time she was prepared.

Using her inherent Type-A tendencies, Samantha had planned this vacation down to a *T*, knew precisely what she wanted and how to go about getting it. Between the combination of the sex diet, her newly improved looks and a beach full of single horny men, surely to God she could find one interested in having a little recreational sex with her. Find one who would know how to do the business properly, so that she would at least be satisfied when it was over. Her lips curled into a slow smile.

Hopefully multisatisfied.

Her gaze strayed to the flyer once more and a prickle of irritation strummed across her frazzled nerves. Just her luck that the one week she'd have the added bonus of diet-induced sex appeal, the beach and B&B would be crawling with tanned, toned and thonged competition.

"Would you like me to call and try to arrange other accommodations for you?" perky Tina asked.

Samantha blinked out of her reverie. "No," she said, exasperated. "I would like to have the accommodations I reserved."

Her smile faltered. "I've told you—"

"I don't care what you've told me," Samantha interrupted tightly. She clawed at her belly, an insistent reminder that she needed those antihistamines now. Her ace-in-the-hole sex diet had one distinctly uncomfortable disadvantage—it primarily consisted of seafood…which she just happened to be mildly allergic to. But desperate times called for desperate measures.

She'd invested—and ingested—too much to turn back now.

Her entire plan hinged on this vacation. She blew out a frustrated breath. "Where's Gladys?" Samantha asked impatiently. Gladys would take care of this snafu and all would be well.

"Somewhere on the Pacific Ocean."

Sam blinked. "What?"

"She got married last week. She's on her honeymoon."

Gladys got married? Crusty old Gladys snagged a husband? Hank had definitely not mentioned that, Samantha thought absently as she managed a sick smile. *That* she would have remembered.

Sam contemplated that disheartening little revelation and wished that she were a big enough person to be happy for Gladys without feeling sorry for herself, but apparently she wasn't, because all she could think was how more pathetic her life seemed now that even Gladys had gotten married.

That settled it, Samantha thought determinedly—she'd get laid this week and have a damned orgasm, or die trying.

"Well, that's nice," Sam finally managed weakly. "What about Hank?"

Another prickle of irritation surfaced. Quite honestly, she'd wanted a minute to freshen up before she saw Hank—a moot point since he didn't care what she looked like—but she couldn't help but look forward to seeing his reaction to her new-and-improved self. She didn't expect him to turn into a lust-crazed maniac—she wasn't stupid enough to even so much as hope that would happen—but a flicker of surprise would be nice. Vain? Yes. But after the effort she put into making herself more attractive, she thought she deserved a little gratification.

Tina blanched. "H-Hank?"

"Yes, Hank," Samantha replied slowly, intrigued by Tina's oh-hell expression.

"Er...he's not here at the moment."

Samantha's eyes narrowed as she watched Tina gnaw nervously on her bottom lip. "I can see that," she said patiently. "Where is he?"

Tina paused, heaved a protracted sigh with a roll of her eyes. "He went to fish a sand crab out of the pool," she admitted begrudgingly, and lifted a small walkie-talkie from the desk. "I'll call him."

From the tone of her voice, a pelvic exam conducted by Captain Hook held more appeal.

Tina depressed the call button and spoke into the black-and-neon-green gadget. "Hank, could you come to the front desk please?"

Static, then, "Is there a problem, Tina?"

Jeez, Samantha thought, just hearing his voice made the fine hairs on her arms stand on end, forced her to repress a shiver. A current of electricity zinged up her spine, tingled her nipples and buzzed her sex with warmth.

Hank Masterson was the epitome of the quintessential beach bum—tall, tanned, built, blond and gorgeous. He had the clearest, most beautiful sea-blue eyes and a lazy, slumberous smile that made a woman's brain melt and her blood simmer. He exuded easy, effortless charm and had cornered the market in sex appeal. In addition to being absolutely gorgeous, he had a great personality and a brilliant head for business. Hank was the total package and if a woman ever managed to hook his attention even for a little while, she had better net him while she could. Men like Hank were few and far between.

And, Samantha thought with a grim, melancholy stab of regret, completely out of her reach.

She might be able to go from geek to chic for a week, but a permanent transformation was more than she could reasonably hope for. Besides, she knew Hank well enough to know that over the years he'd considered her as many things, but regrettably potential girlfriend or lover had never been one of them.

A smile caught the corner of her mouth. The word *nuisance* leapt immediately to mind. As children, Hank had grudgingly tolerated her presence with the sort of martyred stoicism reserved for pesky little girls. But miraculously, by the time she'd reached her teens, she and Hank had developed a very close friendship—one they'd maintained over the years via e-mail, phone calls and yearly visits—and she would have liked nothing better than to parlay that special connection into something more.

Hank, though, had never been remotely interested.

Her lips twisted with wry humor. Hell, if it hadn't been for that ill-fated almost-kiss, she wouldn't have been convinced he'd even noticed that she was a girl. God knows, he'd always treated her just like one of the guys. He'd never displayed the least amount of modesty around her, had routinely stripped and gone skinny-dipping right in front of her drooling, flaming face and, oftentimes, had even shared intimate details of his relationships with other women with her. Things, she was sure, he shared with his male cronies. Items that had made her squirm with longing and jealousy, made her want to break things and scream.

Of course, she'd never done any of those things. She'd always smiled, listened and teased and been her typically amiable self because she'd rather be flayed alive and dipped in boiling oil than to admit her feelings were anything more than platonic, that she'd wanted more from him than a chuck under the chin or a friendly pat on the back. Samantha knew that if Hank ever discovered her true feelings for him, she'd go from being his friend to an object of pity—which was completely intolerable.

When she'd first considered the sex diet, for one blazingly beautiful dramatic moment, Samantha had allowed herself the luxury of dreaming that it would work on him—after all, being drunk almost had—that he would take one look at her, be utterly bowled over by his attraction for her, that he'd curse himself for a fool for never realizing what a prize she was.

Then she'd burnt herself with the curling iron and reason had returned—if he hadn't figured out what a prize she was after all this time, realistically, what were the chances of that happening now?

None.

She'd long ago resigned herself to be content with the relationship they had. She'd wasted enough time lamenting what might have been and had decided to put the remainder of her energy into an attainable goal—finding a lover for this week who would and could induct her into the *Big O Hall of Fame.*

Hank could, without a doubt—just thinking about it made her thighs quiver with repressed longing—but there was a huge difference between *could* and *would,* and she knew he *wouldn't.*

"We have a small reservation error, yes," Tina glumly admitted.

"Another one?" Samantha detected a slight hint of annoyance in his tone.

Tina closed her eyes miserably. "Yes."

A deep sigh, then, "All right. I'll be right there."

Clearly hers wasn't the only booking error dear

Tina had flubbed up, Samantha thought and offered up a sympathetic smile.

Tina's nervous gaze found hers. "He'll be here in a minute."

Samantha nodded, confident that Hank would see to this mess, and absently scratched the inside of her arm. She was quickly running out of time—she needed an antihistamine and a shrimp-cocktail snack. More blasted seafood, the main ingredient of this damned diet. Besides, every moment spent standing at this desk was a moment she could be using to size up possible lovers, officially put her diet to the test.

Her lips curled. Who knew? With a little pheromone therapy and a little luck, hopefully she'd score.

HANK MASTERSON DEFTLY DEPOSITED a crab onto open sand away from the pool area and made his way back around the front of the house to handle another Tina screwup. God, how he missed good old dependable Gladys. Gladys, who despite her cranky nature and the cigarette perpetually crammed in the corner of her mouth, could work the computer reservation system blindfolded and handle any crisis—real or imagined—without his input.

But all good things eventually come to an end and the old adage had held true with his help, because Gladys had been wooed away from Clearwater by a man who had more to offer her than Hank—a few million and a yacht. Hank had hired Gladys's granddaughter as a favor—*"She'll be fantastic!"* Gladys had assured—and he'd wrongfully assumed that efficiency and competence would run in the family.

Not so.

So far Tina had fried two top-of-the-line computer systems, had lost his backup copies of past guest registers and had managed to single-handedly sabotage every electronic device save the walkie-talkies since she arrived. Hank figured it was only a matter of time before those went, too.

The only thing that saved her from a pink slip was the fact that, despite her penchant for tearing things up, she was very personable, had good phone skills…and she was related to Gladys. Hank sighed. He couldn't in good conscience fire Tina, when her grandmother had been like a second mother to him over the past several years.

Still, Hank thought as irritation pulled at a muscle near his mouth, there were times—like now— when the idea held immense appeal. Between wrapping up the busy season and this godforsaken *Belle of the Beach* contest, things on his little stretch of sand were really hopping. He needed a dependable desk clerk. He didn't have a single bed left and he'd had to call in a temp agency to assist his overworked kitchen staff. A full house made for a fatter bank account, so other than being pleasantly exhausted—and having a receptionist from hell—he really couldn't complain. Hank blew out a breath, loped up the front porch steps and emptied the sand out of his shoes. All in all he—

"Hi, Hank," Candy, one of the *Belle* contestants, called from the front porch swing.

Hank stilled for a fraction of a second, morphed a wince into an amiable smile and returned the greeting. Candy wore a come-pump-me grin and her eyes glittered with blatant invitation. Despite the fact that he'd ignored every suggestive overture and turned down the opportunity to see her tattoo several times over the past couple of days, Candy nonetheless continued to stalk him. Considering the fact that she wore a bikini which bared all but her nipples and narrowly covered her crotch, Hank grimly suspected the tattoo was on a part of her anatomy best avoided.

As a rule, he avoided all female guests at the B&B who seemed interested in pursuing a little recreational vacation sex. It wasn't good for business. There were too many other available women in the world to take an unnecessary risk and so far he'd never been uncontrollably tempted. Tempted? Yes. But beyond the scope of his control? No.

Granted things had been harder this week, what with the half-naked gorgeous *Belle* contestants parading along his stretch of sand. But he could handle it. He pushed into the foyer, felt the welcome blast of cool air from the air conditioner. In a few days this contest would be over and he'd have the time to find a suitable partner, one not on his guest roster and not affiliated with this damned contest. He'd simply have to wait it out and—

Hank's thoughts fractured and his step faltered as his gaze landed on the most delectable backside he'd ever seen.

Sweet Lord, he thought as perspiration suddenly dotted his upper lip and a bolt of heat threatened to incinerate his groin, *another hottie.*

Hell, she didn't even have to turn around for him to know that she was absolutely gorgeous and absolutely, unequivocally hot. A mass of light-red curls tumbled sexily over her shoulders and down her slim back. She had a tiny waist, nicely flared hips and legs up to there. Unlike every other woman around here, she had no tan to speak of and her skin glowed with a pale, peachy health. A sweet fruity scent assaulted his senses, *her* scent he knew, and the very essence of that smell triggered something hot, wild and primal within him. Curiously it seemed vaguely familiar.

Pure unadulterated lust chugged through his veins, sped purposefully toward his groin. His skin prickled and his mouth parched. She was temptation on legs and every instinct he had went on full-tilt red alert, causing a roaring through his head. This went beyond the typical run of the mill lust, was somehow sharper, keener, more intense. Less manageable, Hank thought ominously.

There was only one remedy for an attraction like this, Hank thought grimly—absolute quarantine.

He'd have to avoid her like the damned plague.

She turned around then and recognition sucker-punched him, driving every bit of breath from his lungs. Hank felt his eyes bug and his jaw drop. The roaring he'd heard just seconds before ceased abruptly and was replaced with a screeching howl akin to a jet engine gearing up for takeoff. His vision blackened around the edges as he pulled her familiar face into sharp focus.

Samantha McCafferty?

2

SAMANTHA SMILED WARMLY and breathed an audible sigh of relief, then rushed across the foyer and gave him a tight hug. Hank reacted automatically, hugged her back, though he still felt like the world had been turned upside down.

"Hank, thank God. There's been some sort of mix-up and apparently my room isn't available." She drew back and those twinkling green eyes gazed up at him. "Please tell me you can fix this."

"Samantha? Sam?" Hank said, still in a state of slack-jawed shock over her transformation. The rest of the room swelled back into view, but he still felt like he'd been knocked over the head with an anvil.

"Yeah, it's me," she confirmed with a small shrug, not the least bit offended. She did a delightful pirouette, then looked back up and met his gaze. "I, uh, gained a little weight."

She'd gained more than a little weight, Hank thought as his breath once again evacuated his lungs—she'd gained one helluva figure. My God...she had breasts. He blinked, swallowed, blinked again. Great breasts that lay under her tank top like a couple of lush, ripe peaches. And that wasn't the only change, either, Hank noted as he continued to stare at her in openmouthed amazement. She'd lost the glasses and her light green eyes sparkled with amusement and something else, something mysterious and not so easily read. Something almost...wicked.

In the dimmest recesses of his mind a warning bell sounded, but he was too stunned to pay it any heed.

In addition to that, her hair no longer looked like it had had an unfortunate accident with an electrical outlet. Her curls were still tight, yet soft and tumbled over her shoulders like long strands of curly ribbons. Which seemed appropriate, considering she looked like a delectable gift, ready to be opened.

She'd always been beautiful to him—Sam was gorgeous to anyone who took the time to notice because, despite popular opinion, true beauty was something that couldn't be measured aesthetically. It came from within, was the sum total of the entire package. His gaze drifted over her once more. But he'd be a liar if he said he wasn't affected by the outward changes. He was a guy after all and every guy responded to visual stimuli. Not that he'd needed any additional reason to want her—he'd been secretly in lust with her for years—from the summer she turned eighteen to be exact.

Hank scratched his temple, tried to gather his scattered wits. "Fix what again?" he asked, still bewildered.

Then it hit him. Her room. First week of September. God, how could he have forgotten? he thought, mentally smacking his forehead. He'd talked to her just a couple of weeks ago, had been looking forward to her coming down. Her visits were one of the brightest spots of his year. Hank scowled. It was this damned *Belle of the Beach* contest. He hadn't had time—

"My room," Sam repeated. "According to Tina, I don't have a room. Which isn't possible because I have a standing reservation. Right?"

Yes, Hank thought hesitantly, she should…but he had a terrible suspicion that she didn't. A knuckle of unease nudged his belly. "Er…let me take a look."

He moved behind the counter, searched the system for Samantha's reservation and, just as he'd grimly suspected, she didn't have one.

Hank winced, rubbed the back of his neck and gave her a regretful smile. "It's not here." He shot Tina a pointed look. "We've had some computer problems lately."

"Hank," Samantha all but wailed, scratching the inside of her wrist. "What am I going to do? It never occurred to me to call and verify my reservation. I talked to you a couple of weeks ago, remember?'' She blew out a breath, cast him a glance. ''When will the people who are in my room be leaving?''

Hank checked, braced his arms against the counter. His blew out a breath. ''Not until Sunday.''

''Oh, hell.'' She shifted, seemingly at a loss. ''What about any of other rooms? Will any of them come available?''

Hank made a show of checking, but knew the answer to that without looking. ''We're booked solid.''

She swore, rubbed a hand over her elbow.

Hank frowned. ''Is something wrong?''

She arched a brow pointedly. ''You mean aside from the fact that I don't have a room, friend?''

''Yeah.'' He gestured to her hand. ''You're scratching.''

She immediately stilled and flushed like a kid who'd been caught with a hand in the cookie jar. ''No, nothing is wrong…except for the fact that I'm tired and hungry and I've been looking forward to this vacation all year. Which, I distinctly recall telling you in a recent e-mail,'' she added pointedly. She pushed a hand through her curly locks. ''God, I can't believe this is happening.''

A deeper explanation lurked behind that guilt-provoking excuse, but Hank didn't have any idea what on earth it could be. He studied her thoughtfully. Something else was at work here. Still, she was right. Given the recent reservation screwups, he should have checked and made sure that hers were secure. He just hadn't thought about it. Things had been too damned crazy.

She rolled her eyes, then heaved a dramatic put-upon sigh. "Well, if you'll help me get my bags back out to my rental car, I guess I'll head straight back the airport." She moved to pick up a bag.

"No, you won't," Hank heard himself say. "You can stay with me."

She straightened slowly. "What?"

"You'll stay with me." So much for avoiding her like the plague, Hank thought, but then what choice did he really have? This was *Sam.* He couldn't let her leave. And he didn't want her to. Having her here this week would be the only thing that would make it bearable.

Her brow puckered. "Where?"

"In my room," he said patiently, nonchalantly because that was how he was supposed to feel, how a friend would feel. But he didn't—not by any stretch of the imagination. There was nothing patient or nonchalant about the blood sizzling in his crotch. He'd had a hard enough time battling his lust over the years without her turning vamp on him. It was a nasty turn of events, but he'd simply have to deal with it. He'd had a lot of practice, after all.

Her expression grew comically blank. "Your room?"

Despite his present turmoil, Hank chuckled. "Have you developed some sort of hearing disability that I'm unaware of? Of course, my room," he said with mock exasperation. "Where else? You can have the bed. I'll take the couch."

"But you hate that couch."

He heaved a dramatic put upon sigh, tried to look humble. "All the more reason you should appreciate the sacrifice."

A reluctant grin tugged at her lips. "I'd forgotten just how full of sh—"

"Shining light and goodness I am, I know," he finished magnanimously. He sighed deeply. "Just say thank you, and it'll all be worth it."

Her eyes twinkled. "Thank you."

The issue settled, he smacked his hand against the counter. "Besides, you're probably saving my life," he added grimly.

"How so?"

He shot her a look. "Mom and Pop would kill me if I let you leave."

Her eyes suddenly glittered with a warm, knowing humor and her lips curled into a distracting smile. "In that case, I'd hate to be the cause of your untimely demise. How are the pioneers, anyway?"

With effort, Hank forced his gaze away from that ripe mouth. It was unusually carnal, a fact he'd noticed many years ago when he'd almost made the monumental mistake of kissing her. Sam had always been the one woman he could trust, could bare his soul to, could confide in. She was his sounding board, his voice of reason, and was always good for a laugh.

For lack of any better explanation, he liked himself when he was with her, and he couldn't say that about anyone else. Theirs had been the ideal relationship. His feelings for her had always been strictly platonic, there'd been nothing remotely sexual about it—until the summer she turned eighteen.

Hank could still remember the moment his interest had shifted, could still feel that terrifying combination of affection and lust as sharply today as he had the afternoon it had happened. He and Sam had taken the ferry over to Dauphin Island, for what reason exactly, he couldn't remember now. But the trip back—that was one he'd never forget. He and Sam had been standing side by side—a pose as natural as breathing—had been leaning against the railing watching the surf lap at the hull of the boat. He'd caught a glance of her from the corner of his eye—the soft slope of her cheek, that woefully familiar smile, and just like that—in the blink of an eye—his feelings had changed. He'd been hit with the nearly blinding urge to kiss her right then.

But he hadn't.

He and Sam had a good relationship and he'd

had no intention of letting something as fickle as lust screw it up. Not now, not ever. Though it had almost happened once. Drink had dulled his determination and, though common sense had prevailed in the end, he'd almost kissed her and ruined everything.

Since then, he'd never let his guard down, had learned to keep the attraction under control. He slid a glance over her and felt his mood turn grim. A premonition of dread resonated in his belly. Undoubtedly it would be more difficult now.

"The pioneers are fine," he managed to say belatedly in answer to her question. The thought of his Mom and Dad drew a smile.

His parents had taken an Alaskan cruise for their thirty-fifth wedding anniversary, had fallen in love with the Last Frontier and decided to turn the B&B over to him and head off to Alaska. Though he enjoyed running the B&B, he still missed them terribly. During the off season, he made regular visits, however those small bits of time never seemed like enough to catch up.

"That's good to hear," she said, then bit her bottom lip. "Are you absolutely certain that you don't mind if I stay with you? I could take the couch. Or try to find another hotel."

Hank shook his head. "Don't be ridiculous. You'll stay here. Let me get your bags and I'll show you to…our room."

Hank came around the counter, hefted Samantha's bags and gestured for her to follow him down the hall. That fruity, mantrap scent swirled around his head once more, making his nerve-endings hum and his blood sizzle. He blinked, feeling almost dazed, then mentally swore and shook off the sensation.

He looked back at her from over his shoulder and her absolute beauty slammed into him once more.

She'd mentioned in passing conversation over the past year that she'd made some changes to herself, had been spending a lot of time at the gym, but he'd never dreamed that this would have been the end result.

He should have known better.

That's what he'd always liked about Samantha. No bullshit. Yes meant yes and no meant no, and he never had to worry about being politically correct or any of that other crap. He could just be himself with all his little idiosyncrasies and imperfections, and know that she wouldn't pass judgment. Furthermore, when she set out to do something, she did it. Failure with her was simply not an option. Still… "What kind of perfume are you wearing?"

A frown wrinkled her brow. "None. Why?"

Hank turned back around, continued down the hall to the back of the house. "You smell good. Fruity. Sweet."

She hummed under her breath. "Must be my fabric softener."

Some fabric softener, Hank thought. It made him want to rip her clothes off.

He was suddenly hit with the insane urge to slide his hands over her newfound curves, taste her ripe, peachy breasts and sample that utterly carnal mouth of hers, to fasten his mouth on her sex and see if that hot slick valley between her thighs smelled as sweet and fruity as the rest of her. To see if it tasted as sweet as she smelled.

Hank squeezed his eyes shut and, with extreme effort, derailed that demented train of thought. This was not good, he thought as he slipped the key in the lock. A mixture of anticipation and doom congealed in his belly as he pushed the door open and ushered her into his room.

So much for the quarantine, Hank thought numbly. Unless he wanted to move out of his house, he wouldn't have a prayer of avoiding her. And the hell of it was...he didn't want to.

SAMANTHA COVERTLY SCRATCHED the underside of her arm as Hank busied himself with opening the door. The minute she got into this room, she would have to excuse herself to the bathroom and pop an antihistamine before it was too late and these mere tingling irritations turned into full-blown hives. That would not be good, and the last thing she needed was for Hank to become suspicious. Samantha inwardly shuddered. She would die of mortification and embarrassment if he ever found out the lengths she'd gone to in order to get her rightfully deserved orgasm. Quite honestly, being strip-searched by a butch lesbian with a billy club fetish held greater appeal.

Hank walked across the gleaming hardwood and dropped her bags at the foot of his rumpled four-poster bed. ''I'll clean out a couple of drawers and see if I can make some room for you in the closet.''

''Thanks.'' She jerked her thumb toward the en suite bath. ''I've got to…''

Hank nodded succinctly. ''Sure.'' He glanced around the room, winced, then shoved a hand through his sun-bleached hair. ''I'll straighten up a little bit, too.''

''Still not letting housekeeping in?'' Samantha said as she carefully picked her way over dirty clothes and orphaned shoes. She remembered that he'd always been a slob, and frankly, found the idea ridiculously endearing. Of course, she probably wouldn't if she had to clean up after him.

''Nah,'' he replied, absently gathering trash from the nightstand. ''I can't ever find anything after they've been in here.''

Samantha grinned and let herself into the bathroom, then sagged against the closed door.

Sweet Lord. No matter how many times she saw

Hank, no matter how many times she told herself that this time things would be different—she wouldn't be so affected by him—she always felt like the wind had been knocked from her sails, felt the ground shift beneath her feet. A curious buzzing sounded in her head and a hot sweet rush of affection and desire flooded her, pushing an instant smile to her lips. She'd undoubtedly looked like a goofy geek—she couldn't help it, that's who she was—but she'd never been able to pretend to be less than thrilled when she saw him. She simply couldn't help herself.

When he'd strolled into the foyer looking like he'd just stepped off the set of *Baywatch* and immediately flashed that gorgeous, oh-so-lazy smile at her, it had been all Samantha could do to keep her watery knees from buckling. That achy place between her legs had throbbed and her nipples had tingled. She'd always been in lust with him—show her a female who wasn't and she'd show you a liar—but the sensation had been altogether sharper, keener. A product of this sex diet, no doubt.

In addition to her howling, woefully neglected hormones, she'd eaten enough shellfish, kelp, pine nuts, honey and any other known aphrodisiac to sink a ship in the past three days. It was only natural that her desire would be sharper, more intense. Truthfully, she wouldn't have thought it was possible.

Over the past year, she'd been a sexually frustrated wreck, had even gone so far as to consider hiring a man for the night—anything was possible in Aspen, for the right price. But there had been something so pathetic about paying a man to sleep with her that she hadn't been able to go through with it. Granted she was running a risk doing things this way—she might end up with a dud and wind up as unfulfilled as she'd been during the first go round.

With a professional, that wouldn't have happened. She could have insisted on a money-back guarantee. The idea drew a slow smile. Still, it had just been too depressing to pay for sex. She'd take her chances with the sex diet. She only wanted an orgasm, after all, and she had absolutely no illusions about falling in love.

Sam inwardly snorted. She'd given up on that pipe dream. Regardless of how great she looked now—and, dammit, she did look pretty good, if she did say so herself—she didn't know if she'd be able to keep up the maintenance. It took a lot of effort to be pretty. Hair gel, plucking, tweezing, moisturizing, makeup and protein shakes.

She knew the effort was worth the reward—she certainly felt a lot better about herself when she knew she looked good. Still, sometimes it just seemed like too much. Unfortunately she hadn't been born one of those women who could roll out of bed and look gorgeous *au naturel*. Samantha smirked, tossed an antihistamine into her mouth and chased it with a sip of water. Regrettably, she needed all the help she could get.

Thus, the sex diet.

It made her more appealing to the opposite sex and, when combined with her plan, practically guaranteed her success. Better still, whomever she finally invited into her bed would actually want to be with her—unlike a male escort, who would smile and compliment her and do all of the wonderfully wicked things she longed to experience—but with an agenda. It would be for the cash, not the act, and that was the difference. That was what she hadn't been able to stomach. She'd have all of those things and more—she'd have a man who genuinely wanted her.

At least until she went off the diet.

The only fly in the ointment, but she was past caring. She wanted—*needed*—to get laid.

As long as she followed through with her plan— she'd consulted every how-to-hook-a-man book and sex manual she could get her hands on, as well as faithfully read every trendy magazine that offered tips on dating and sex—she didn't see how things could go wrong. Furthermore, she'd learned everything that men *didn't* like from Hank. Years of listening to him bemoan certain female behavior had left her with a better understanding than most of what a man might look for in a temporary partner.

And, as an added bonus, she felt at home here, in her element and comfortable enough with the clientele along this end of the beach to know that she couldn't go terribly wrong with whomever she chose.

In addition to packing a few key snacks for her diet, she'd brought along an arsenal of various protection. She'd prepared for this week like a general prepared for war. She was ready. Past ready. Hell, it was unnatural for a woman her age to have never had an orgasm, to have never experienced the legendary *Big O*.

Samantha swallowed a frustrated groan. She wanted to get laid—properly! She wanted to know what it felt like to have a man's mouth feeding at her breast—Ted, her lackluster first and only, hadn't even bothered to cop a feel, had moved with alarming rapidity to the grand finale.

Sam wanted someone to make love to her, to feel a man's body, his hard weight against hers, have him touch that secret place inside her that throbbed from neglect. She wanted to know what all the fuss was about. Why so many books, shows and magazines made such a tremendous deal about doing it right, doing it wrong, the where, the when, the how and the who.

She'd been with a guy who'd done it wrong—

she wanted to be with a guy who would do it right. It wasn't too much to ask.

Hank's handsome image loomed instantly to mind. Frankly she'd like nothing better than to experience it with him, but knew that no matter what she'd shocked him with her new and improved self—she most definitely had. Gratifyingly, his jaw had dropped and she'd seen a true glimmer of male interest flicker before realization had snuffed it out.

She knew that no matter how much she'd changed and despite the fact that he'd noticed those changes, he'd still look at her and remember the frizzy hair, freckles, bottle-bottom glasses and scrawny body. Sadly, to him, no matter how many improvements she made physically, he'd always look at her and see an ugly duckling, not the swan she'd managed to turn herself into.

He'd always see a friend, not a potential lover.

Samantha stared glumly at her reflection and a pang of regret pricked her heart, but she determinedly squelched the sentiment. There would be no regrets on this trip. This trip was going to be the most memorable week of her life and she wasn't about to let a little thing like unrequited lust—or love, as the case may be—get in the way.

After all, she had bigger fish to fry. Her lips quirked with perverse humor.

But first she'd need to eat some.

3

SHE CAUGHT HANK KICKING a pile of dirty clothes against the wall when she came out of the bathroom. He looked up and those bright eyes glittered with sheepish humor. "I made a foot of space available in the closet, and those top two drawers in the dresser are ready." He passed a hand over his face. "I really hate what happened about your room. Things have been crazy around here since Gladys left. Tina will eventually get it." His voice sounded more grim than hopeful, making Samantha's lips twitch. "But between her frequent screwups and this *Belle of the Beach* contest, I've been stretched pretty thin."

Samantha waved off his concern. "Don't worry about it." She conjured a playful grin. "I'm sure I'll be perfectly comfortable in your bed."

Of course, she'd be more comfortable if he were in it with her, but that wasn't a likely scenario so she needed to put the idea out of her head. If she didn't, she might as well kiss that orgasm goodbye. She cast a glance at the smallish couch and tried to imagine Hank's big muscular frame sprawled over it. She winced. "But I don't know how comfortable you'll be."

Hank grinned, slouched casually against the bedpost. "I'll consider it penance for screwing up your reservation."

"With that sort of logic, I should have gotten Tina's bed."

Hank grunted. "Trust me, if she lived in the house, she'd be giving up her bed ten times over."

Samantha winced. "That bad, eh?"

He nodded, blew out a breath. "That bad."

"If she's so horrible, then why do you keep her?"

"She's Gladys's granddaughter."

"Oh," Samantha said knowingly. That explained it. Hank adored Gladys. He'd never do anything that might hurt her, even if it meant he paid the price for it. In this case, *literally*. An inept desk clerk in his line of work could be devastating. Still... "She didn't train her before she left?"

"She tried." Hank lifted one shoulder in a negligent shrug. "Said that no amount of training would be better than on-the-job experience."

Translation: Tina didn't get it and Gladys had given up. Poor Hank, Samantha thought, not envying his predicament. "So what's the deal with this *Belle of the Beach* contest?" she asked after a moment. "I saw a flyer next to the front desk."

Hank crossed his arms over his chest, rolled his eyes and snorted. "It's hell."

"Surely it's not that bad. Business certainly seems to be booming."

Hank blew out a heavy breath, rubbed a hand over his face. "It is, and it's all due to the pageant. Nevertheless, I wish that Mayor Flannagin could have come up with another way to boost the end-season besides this." He rolled his eyes. "Hell, *anything* but this."

"Funny," Samantha said. She arched a brow and regarded him with amusement. "I would have thought that a bunch of gorgeous women on your sand would have been right up your alley."

He flashed a smile, unwittingly kicking her pulse into overdrive. "Me, too, but it's not." His alto-gether-too-hot gaze did a lengthy sweep over her body, causing a tornado of tingles in her belly. "You should enter."

A nervous flutter winged through her chest. She tucked a strand of hair behind her ear. "Nah," she hedged. "I'm not the beauty pageant type."

"You might be surprised," Hank told her. "Be-sides, this is no ordinary pageant." His amused gaze tangled with hers. "'There's more to being a *Belle* than just a pretty face.'"

Samantha grinned, recognizing the line from the flyer. "Is that right?"

"That's right," he told her, warming to his subject. "The official contest kicks off tomorrow and secret judges will be milling around grading contestants on personality, charm, grace and graciousness. The final contestants will compete in *Redneck Jeopardy*. And there's no swimsuit competition. Instead Belle contestants will have a fried chicken and iced tea cook off."

"What?"

He nodded and poked his tongue in his cheek. "You heard me," he repeated, laughing. "Hell, every southern belle should know how to fry chicken and make iced tea."

"That is so sexist," Samantha replied, appalled.

A deep, wholly sexy laugh rumbled up his throat. "Take it up with Mayor Flannagin. This was his brainchild."

Smiling, Samantha shook her head. "Unbelievable. Simply unbelievable." Still, she wasn't surprised. This was exactly the sort of thing she could expect from her little hometown. It was as exasperating as it was endearing.

"Yeah, well, an unbelievable prize package goes to the winner. An all-expenses-paid trip for two to the Bahamas, a fully loaded SUV and ten grand in cash." The corner of his mouth tucked into a grin. "Hard to beat that. The contest committee decided to keep the entry fee minimal in order to increase participation." He shrugged lazily. "More entries, more tourists. More tourists, more money."

Made sense, she supposed. Still, a fried chicken and iced tea contest? Please.

Hank pushed away from the bedpost. "There are entry forms at the front desk and registration ends today," he said, matter-of-factly. "You should enter. What have you got to lose?"

To her absolute amazement, she found herself seriously considering it. She might not be the most gorgeous woman here, but she was definitely intelligent, had a pretty good personality, considered herself charming and gracious. Anticipation hummed along her nerves as the idea gained momentum. As for talent, she was no Mariah Carey, but could sing a decent ballad. And, thanks to her mother, she could fry one helluva chicken. She certainly wouldn't be a shoo-in, Samantha thought consideringly, but she had a shot. She definitely had a shot.

Furthermore, she could use a new car, had always wanted to travel and she could definitely use the cash. If she added ten grand to her nest egg, she could go ahead and move back home. Could be close to Hank. It would be tight, but she could still do it. Her insides grew jittery with cautiously hopeful excitement.

Hank was right. What did she have to lose?

Samantha bit her lip, looked up and her gaze bumped into his. "Forms are at the front desk?"

"Yeah."

"I think I'll change into my suit, grab a bite to eat out by the pool and look it over."

He nodded, seemingly pleased. "Good." He paused. "It's great to have you back, Sam. You, uh, look fantastic," he added, looking somewhat uncomfortable. And no wonder—he'd never had cause to issue a compliment before.

Her heart warmed all the same and she flashed him a smile. "It's great to be back."

"Any particular plans for this vacation?" he asked lightly. "A trip to Dauphin Island? Fort Morgan?"

Those were her usual haunts when she came to town, but *Operation Orgasm* wasn't going to leave her much time for those pursuits. "Nah, no plans per se," Samantha said evasively, unwilling to meet his gaze lest he discover her true intentions. Which was ridiculous. Why did she care if he knew what she was about? He'd never hesitated to share his plans about women with her. He'd always been heartbreakingly honest about his lovers.

Samantha moved to the foot of the bed, opened a suitcase and fished her bikini from one of the front pockets. She tossed it on the bed, then dug around for her sunblock. Unless she wanted to fry and freckle, she had to cover herself in SPF thirty-five. She was fair complexioned, but could turn sort of peachy if she played her cards right. She'd primed her skin last week with a few trips to the tanning bed, so hopefully she wouldn't burn.

She could feel Hank's gaze on her, could feel him studying her, checking for a secret via retinal scrutiny. "When you say per se…just exactly what do you mean?"

Where the hell was her sunblock, Samantha wondered, growing slightly annoyed. She knew she'd packed it. Remembered shoving it into the bag. She pilfered around a little more, nudged various items aside. Exasperated, she jerked a couple of magazines and small boxes out of the pocket, absently set them aside. Honestly, this was ridiculous. She knew she'd packed the damned—

Hank's wicked chuckle interrupted her irritating quest. Something about that laugh made her spine prickle with foreboding.

When she looked up, he held her bikini bottoms in one hand and a box of glow-in-the-dark extra-large condoms in the other. "Care to explain?" he asked.

Though she longed for the floor to open up and swallow her—knew that her cheeks were blazing with embarrassment—Samantha managed to force a smile, lifted her shoulders in an exaggerated shrug and huffed a dramatic sigh. "Well, if I need to, I will. Though I must confess I would have thought that a man your age would have a general idea of what condoms were used for. In fact, I distinctly remember you carrying one in your wallet back—''

He smirked. ''Cute. But that's not what I meant.'' His eyes narrowed and he twirled her bikini bottoms around his index finger. ''Since when are you packing enough rubbers to outfit the defensive line at the state college?''

Samantha straightened and calmly snatched her prophylactics from his unsuspecting hand, then shoved them back into her suitcase. She requisitioned her bikini bottoms as well, then grabbed the top.

''Since I started having sex,'' she replied, mildly annoyed at his somewhat shocked look. He didn't have to look so damned dumbfounded, like the idea of her having sex—or anyone wanting to have sex with her—was out of the scope of his imagination. It undermined her confidence.

''Since you started having sex?'' he asked slowly. His voice had developed a dry rasp and that smug smile he'd worn just a second ago had capsized. His eyes suddenly widened in horrified understanding. ''My God, you're trolling, aren't you? You're—''

''And I've got more than enough to outfit the defensive line at state college, smart ass—I have enough for the offensive line and special teams as well.'' She smiled. ''Just let me know if you need to borrow any. Of course, I only carry extra-large—'' she purposely let her gaze drop to the front of his shorts ''—so they might not fit.''

His jaw went comically slack.

Samantha grinned, heartened by his stunned expression. ''As for trolling—'' she shrugged lazily ''—I might throw out a line or two. Now if you'll excuse me, I'm going to change.''

THERE WASN'T ANY ''GOING TO'' about it, Hank thought as he covertly watched Samantha entertain a host of bastards—all of them on pussy patrol, by the looks of them—at her table by the pool.

She *had* changed.

The Samantha he'd known all of his life would have never had the nerve to wear that bikini—honestly, she might as well be naked for everything that it covered, which was precious little, Hank thought feeling a smidge light-headed as he watched her peachy breasts nearly tumble out of the satiny push-up cups. One more sexy laugh like that, and that top was going to go, Hank thought ominously. His mouth watered at the mere thought.

After the Great Condom Discovery, Hank had decided to station himself by the pool and keep an eye out on her. Obviously she'd decided to cast out more than a line or two, he thought grimly—she'd lowered a sizable net.

Samantha McCafferty had to be one of the most practical, sensible women he'd ever known—she wouldn't have packed a damned arsenal of rubbers unless she fully intended to use them.

She was going to have sex.

Had been having sex.

The mere idea set his teeth on edge, made his skin itch, made his brain feel entirely too small for his skull. The physical changes combined with the condoms and a couple of headlines he'd read from the magazines she'd pulled out of her suitcase—''Getting Lucky—Tips From The Pros'' and ''The Big O—How To Make Your Lover Go From A Dud to a Stud''—had led him to the unhappy conclusion that she planned to take a lover this week. A tic formed near his left eye.

No wonder she'd been so upset about not having her room, Hank thought. Evidently she'd gone to a lot of trouble to plan this vacation sex-fest and Tina's screwup had mucked up her carefully laid plans.

God bless Tina, Hank thought, vastly relieved. For once, her ineptness had worked in his favor.

Hank realized that Samantha was an adult and should have the freedom to conduct her life in any way that she saw fit...but he didn't care. Crass? Obnoxious? Selfish? Politically incorrect? All of the above. But he still didn't care. The only thing he cared about at present was stopping her. There was no way in hell he'd be able to stand idly by and watch her waltz off into the sunset with some other guy. For reasons he had no intention of exploring, the idea of any man touching her made a hot, red haze swim before his eyes, made his stomach cramp with an emotion mortifyingly like jealousy. Made him want to hurl chairs into the pool and beat the living hell out of someone. His eyes narrowed. The guys currently swarming around her like a hive of horny bees, stingers at the ready, looked like perfect targets.

This was horrible. That first premonition of dread he'd experienced had morphed into a sickening ulcer in the pit of his stomach. Keeping this secret attraction under control would be hard enough in normal circumstances, but when he factored in her being in his room, that delightful new figure, and her obvious intentions for the week, he had to forcibly quell the urge to tear out his hair.

Furthermore—and it really ate at him to admit it—but if she'd gone to all the trouble to plan a seduction, why hadn't she decided to seduce him? Hank wondered, unreasonably irritated. Why hadn't she considered *him* as a possible candidate? A potential lover?

He stilled and swore hotly.

Which was the exact opposite of what he should have been thinking. A seduction would ruin everything, was the exact scenario he'd worked so hard to avoid. And it had been hard, dammit. Harder than she would ever know. But it would be the end of a lifelong friendship—one he valued tremendously—because nothing changed the dynamic of a relationship quicker than sex.

No matter how much he suffered through the grip of this unholy attraction, he had to keep that in mind. Did he want her? More than his next breath. Had wanted her for years. And in this case, he'd wanted her before he realized who she was, and to his extreme discomfort and ceaseless irritation, wanted her more now than ever.

Her tinkling laughter drifted to him on the salty afternoon breeze and he paused to look at her. A curious ache settled in his chest. The wind sent a long curl brushing along her creamy cheek and she wore a smile of absolute delight. He couldn't see those pale green eyes behind her trendy sunglasses, but knew they'd be crinkled at the corners and glinting with a humor that seemed to literally light her up. She'd always been like that, Hank thought. Infectiously happy. How many times over the years had she shared that with him?

She'd twisted her hair up into some sort of giant claw thing, yet a few stands had worked loose and danced over her nape. Though she'd only been out by the pool for an hour or so, and he'd seen her take the sunblock into the bathroom when she'd gone to change, her slim shoulders were growing slightly pink.

Which seemed appropriate—then her whole body

would match that pink barely there bikini and she'd be giving the illusion of being nude.

Which she more or less was to him and any other man who looked at her.

Hank mentally whistled. God, what a body. Who would have ever thought that a little weight would have made such a difference? And she'd gained every bit of it in all the right places—her breasts, her hips and her ass. She'd filled out and had a perfect petite hourglass figure. He wanted to wrap that red curly strand of hair presently swishing across her cheek around his finger, tug her closer, breathe in that fruity lust-provoking scent and kiss those sexy smiling lips.

Hank was no stranger to lust, knew what the sharp tug felt like. But this was no regular tug—it was an all-consuming yank mixed with a disturbingly tender emotion he didn't readily recognize and he'd never once associated with sex. It was a warning, he knew, a sensation he'd only experienced with Sam, and all the more reason he'd make sure to keep his libido in check.

But what in the hell was he going to do? he wondered, blindsided with another wave of helpless, frustrated panic. He couldn't just sit by and watch those bastards flirt with her. He could practically see her sizing them up, figuring out which one would best serve her purposes—which one would wear an extra-large condom, Hank thought darkly—basking in their attention.

She looked completely at ease, too, not the least bit shy or overwhelmed by all the attention. She dipped a shrimp in cocktail sauce, blithely popped it into her mouth, tossed her head back and laughed at something one of the men said. Something niggled at him, a thought played hide-and-seek in his brain, but he didn't have time to chase it. He had other pressing thoughts to consider—like how to keep her in his bed and out of someone else's.

Hank scowled. By the looks of it, she was thoroughly enjoying herself and if he didn't come up with some sort of plan soon, she'd undoubtedly double-time it to the room, snag her handy stash of condoms and join one of these jerks in his room tonight. She'd be having sex. In his house. And it wouldn't be with him.

His brain cramped at the thought.

He couldn't allow that to happen.

He could not.

She'd used their friendship to finagle her way into his room, Hank thought, more than marginally annoyed now that he knew why she'd been so desperate to stay. Since she'd used that ploy first, Hank decided he wouldn't have any compunction about using that same friendship to *keep* her there.

He grinned. For starters, a let's-catch-up-on-old-times dinner would be in order.

4

SAMANTHA ABSENTLY LAUGHED at something one of the guys said and watched Hank from the corner of her eye. He wore an interesting expression, one she didn't think she'd ever seen on his handsome, carefree face before—a glower.

Those sun-bleached brows were lowered in an intimidating scowl and his usually smiling lips were thinned into a mulish line. She could read irritation in every line of his glorious body, could practically feel his tension from across the pool. He'd been giving everyone around her the evil eye all afternoon, but thankfully none of her new friends/potential lovers had found him all that intimidating. They were, after all, paying customers so he couldn't afford to be blatantly rude. That would hardly be hospitable.

To onlookers around the pool, Hank's behavior might be construed as jealousy, but only she knew better. One had to be interested in order to be jealous, and he certainly wasn't interested in her. A bubble of regret emerged among the irritation simmering in her stomach. No, Hank had seen the condoms, factored in the extreme effort behind her new appearance and had apparently reached a conclusion which had triggered a misplaced rush of belated brotherly protection.

Well, she didn't need protecting, thank you very much—she needed an orgasm—and if he didn't stop glaring at her posthaste, she'd undoubtedly be forced to enlighten him. She instinctively knew he'd be better off in the dark. Nevertheless, she'd put too much thought and work into making herself appealing to the opposite sex to let him come along with misguided, well-meaning intentions and screw it up. Time was of the essence, the clock was ticking and she couldn't afford any distractions.

To her unending delight, this sex diet seemed to be working quite well. She popped another cocktail shrimp into her mouth and silently thanked the marvels of modern medicine which kept her from looking like a giant, blotchy blowfish.

Samantha had scarcely gotten to a table before a guy—Jeff, if memory served—had offered to buy her a drink. She'd opted for a soda. In addition to not mixing alcohol with the antihistamines—a big no-no, she was sure—she wanted all of her wits about her. She liked the warm sluggish pleasure of a buzz as much as anyone, but she'd been cocktailed the last time she'd chosen a lover and the end result had been disastrous, unremarkable and unfulfilling.

She wouldn't make that mistake this time.

This time, she knew exactly what she was doing, and she firmly intended on picking the right guy. A consummate lover, a guy who not only possessed impressive equipment, but knew exactly how to use it. A guy who obviously wasn't looking for anything more than a good time, a meaningless relationship based on mutual attraction and self-gratification. Anticipation sent a thrill rushing through her.

The kind of guy her mother had repeatedly warned her about…the kind that would normally scare her to death.

The idea made something hot and achy slither through her limbs, swirl through her abdomen and settle in her sex. Excitement swept her up in a rush of jitters.

Samantha covertly studied the group around her over the rim of her drink and she felt a smile tease her lips. She had several possible candidates around her right now. With the exception of Carlton, whose mother had called twice on his cell phone in the past hour and who seemed entirely too nice for her purposes, and Ted, whose ring finger bore a distinct white line where his wedding band should be, she still had quite a little pool of could-be lovers huddled gratifyingly around her.

Or she would so long as Hank stayed away, Samantha thought, mildly annoyed, as she wa him determinedly amble closer and closer to where she sat.

He currently strolled from table to table, tending to his duties as host, making sure that each of his guests enjoyed their stay, that accommodations and amenities were up to par. She'd seen him go through the motions on countless occasions, had always envied his natural confidence and charm, the way he never met a stranger and seemed to always know exactly what to say…but there was something distinctly different about the practiced routine this afternoon. There seemed to be a purpose behind that lazy charm and, for reasons which escaped her right now, she got the most overwhelming impression that it had something to do with her.

Samantha watched him, felt the old familiar rush of affection and longing well in her chest and a silent, wistful sigh slipped past her lips. Despite her current irritations, a dozen if-only's skipped through her thoughts.

If only I'd been born beautiful.

If only it could have been you.

If only you could love me…

She blinked, forcing the useless thoughts aside. She didn't have time for if-only's anymore. She'd wasted enough of her life pining over something that was obviously never meant to be and she'd be damned if she'd spend this week mired in muddy regrets.

This week wasn't going to be about what she *couldn't* have, but what she *could*—which was a much needed, competent lover who could deliver her to release, with luck, repeatedly.

Her gaze slid to Jamie, a general contractor from Birmingham. He was tall, dark, handsome and dangerous, if that wicked little curl of his lips was any indication. He had an irreverent yet intense look about him that piqued her curiosity and put him as the lead contender for the moment. She wasn't bowled over by her attraction for him, by any stretch of the imagination, but there was definitely a fizzle of…something. Her lips twitched. He looked fully capable of fanning her flame, that was for sure.

Samantha tuned back into the conversation, hoping to glean a little more information about him. Impatience drew a frown across her brow. If she could just ask him a few pertinent questions, they could skip all of the preliminaries and get to the good stuff. For a second, she imagined herself asking him for a private moment, then launching into a very personal interview.

So, tell me, Jamie, do you consider yourself a good lover? Are you selfish lover? Do you have a clean bill of health? No medical problems, or sexually transmitted diseases? How large is your penis? Were we to sleep together, would you last long enough to make sure that I was completely satis-

*fied? How do you feel about oral sex? How would
you feel about having sex with me all week, then
forgetting me? Does that sound doable? How does
now—*

"I don't know what you're thinking right now,
but from the looks of that lurid little grin, I'd bet
it's X-rated," a deep, familiar voice whispered in
her ear.

Samantha started, cursed the skitter of heat that
blazed down her neck where his breath had fanned
against her. How had he managed to lean in behind
her like that without her knowing? She normally
had great Hank radar, could feel him when he came
near. Still, despite the fact that she was heartily annoyed at him right now, she found herself returning
his grin. That compelling sparkle in his sea-blue
gaze triggered an automatic smile. It always had.

"That's a bet you'd lose," she told him matter-
of-factly. "I'm sure it was only R-rated."

His smile froze for a fraction of a second and,
though it could have been her imagination, he
seemed to wince in pain. "Which one of these los-
ers inspired an R-rated daydream?" he asked in a
low husky voice, so that the others wouldn't hear.

Sam grinned. "That's a need-to-know question,
Hank, and you don't need to know." She leaned
forward, effectively ending their private conversation. "Does everyone know Hank Masterson, our
host?"

Hank shot her a look, then easily moved into host mode. Rather than simply asking the traditional how-are-you, where-are-you-from questions, he smoothly interrogated her little batch of admirers with carefully veiled questions about girlfriends, wives and ex-wives, and one cryptic little comment to the Mama's Boy about a recent stint in rehab until Jamie, her lead contender, was the only one left that Hank hadn't managed to completely discredit. A mixture of annoyance and anxiety festered in her belly.

In fact, though she'd never seen Jamie here at the B&B during any of her visits, she'd gotten the distinct impression that he was not only a regular, but possibly a friend of Hank's. Conversation between the two flowed easily, and a passing reference to a recent surfing excursion, as well as the not-so-subtle way Hank seemed to be warning Jamie away from her—hell, any minute now, she fully expected Hank to drop his pants and mark her damned chair—led her to believe that her suspicions were correct.

Samantha would like to think that the combination of the sex diet and her new-and-improved looks would prevent Jamie from falling for Hank's ploy, but to be honest, she just wasn't that confident. Who knew with men? They played by a mysterious set of rules, rules she'd never understood. She sensed a keen competitive streak in Jamie and fervently prayed it would work in her favor. Still, she'd have been much better off if Hank had simply minded his own business.

Keeping a polite smile on her face while she inwardly seethed with irritation was much more difficult than she would have ever imagined. With a handful of words and fewer minutes, Hank had single-handedly—purposely—wrecked what it had taken her almost an entire year to plan and execute. The protein shakes, the trips to the gym, hours and hours spent in front of the mirror experimenting with makeup and hair gel, then implementing the sex diet. She'd nearly put her eyes out, trying to learn how to put in the damned contact lenses. Samantha ground her teeth as her irritation level morphed into outright anger. She'd forced herself to eat foods that she didn't particularly care for— as well as the ones she was allergic to—all in order to have this one week of sexual bliss, of carnal pleasure. Dammit, it wasn't too much to ask.

She wanted it.

She deserved it.

She *needed* it.

She'd spent years as Responsible Samantha. It had been a rewarding, yet profoundly lonely existence. One week of being reckless out of a lifetime of model behavior wasn't unreasonable, wasn't selfish. She cut Hank a venomously sweet glance. And if he thought that she would let him get away with it—if he thought she'd simply give up because he'd managed to pan this little throng of guys—then he'd better think again. There were plenty of men on this beach, Samantha thought with a determined mental shrug.

She'd simply find more, then narrow it down to one.

"SO THAT'S SAMANTHA," Jamie said thoughtfully. "Funny, she's not at all how I had her pictured."

Hank watched the object of his present turmoil perform a perfect dive from the side of the pool and felt his grim mood plummet into the bleak zone. He grimaced. Passed a hand over his face and snorted. "Me, either."

It had taken several offhand yet casually threatening comments to break up the little gang huddled around her this afternoon, but eventually every guy with the exception of Jamie had slunk off in search of different prey. Jamie, Hank knew, was hanging around to find out what had made him act like a cracked stalker off his meds. He and Jamie hadn't known each other long, but that hadn't stopped them from becoming instant friends. They'd met at an amateur surfing competition and the rest had been history. Jamie had called last week and asked if he could come down. He'd claimed that he had some vacation time built up, but Hank suspected that something else had compelled the hasty visit. What, exactly, he didn't know and he refused to pry to find out. When and if he was ever ready, Jamie would tell him.

But Samantha was a different story—he wasn't beneath prying or anything else for that matter, Hank thought grimly.

She clearly hadn't appreciated his interference—she'd glared at him for the remainder of the afternoon and at one point, under the guise of adjusting her seat to catch more rays, he suspected she'd purposely set her chair down on top of his foot.

Hank had pretended to be baffled by her irritated behavior, but she'd undoubtedly seen right through him. Which was no surprise. Hell, they'd always been able to read each other. He supposed that's why they'd always been such good friends. No beating around the bush and no bullshit. Considering that, he wondered how long it would take her to realize that he wasn't merely trying to keep her from making a mistake, but had a personal interest in keeping those condoms stuffed carefully away in her bag. The mere idea made his stomach cramp and his skin prickle.

He'd realized the minute that he asked her about her plans for the week that something was up. Samantha was a planner by nature. She didn't do anything without making a list, without a strategy. Even if she hadn't tensed up, been deliberately evasive and refused to meet his gaze, he would have known that something was off. He'd bet his life savings that she had a list in her purse, outlining every move she planned to make this week.

Jamie took a long draw from his beer, watched Samantha with the kind of interest that left Hank with the unreasonable urge to plant his fist in his friend's face. "You'd mentioned that she was a nice girl and a good friend. You've talked about her a lot. But what you failed to mention," Jamie said consideringly, "was that she's drop-dead gorgeous."

That's because Sam was his and he didn't want to share her with anyone, including another good friend, Hank thought stubbornly. He grunted in response, unwilling to share the truth.

Jamie leaned farther back into his chair and crossed his feet at his ankles. "So, either you were holding out…or you're indifferent."

Wrong on both counts, Hank thought, with another noncommittal grunt. He hadn't been holding out, and he definitely wasn't indifferent. He'd never been indifferent, not where Sam was concerned. The problem had always been that he cared too much.

He'd watched guys huddle around her all day, stare at her breasts and mouth, fetch and carry and basically jockey for a chance between her thighs. Had watched her laugh and flirt—she'd clearly

loved the attention, which had further irritated him
as she normally reserved that kind of behavior just
for him—and, as the day had progressed, he'd gone
from being disturbingly annoyed to irrationally—
unequivocally—pissed. Pissed at himself for being
in lust with her, pissed at her for making him feel
that way, and pissed at every man—Hank shot a
dark look at Jamie—including his good friend, for
hovering around her all day like starving dogs waiting for scraps at the back door of a meat market.

He didn't know what precisely had prompted this
sudden sex-quest of hers, but knew that it could
only end in heartache for her and eternal frustration
for himself.

He couldn't let that happen.

Hell, if she wanted to get laid that desperately,
she could damn well do it in Colorado. She didn't
have to do it here, right under his nose, for chris-
sakes. He passed a hand over his face. Curiously
the idea of her doing it in Aspen held even less
appeal than her doing it here, and it occurred to
Hank that he'd just as soon her not do it at all.
Unless it was with him, which was as unacceptable
as it was unreasonable.

He *could not* sleep with Samantha…which
begged the arrogant assumption that she wanted to
sleep with him when, clearly, she didn't. He
scowled. Otherwise, she'd be flashing her cleavage
at him, not at everyone else.

Jamie shot him a sidelong glance, then returned his attention to Samantha, who'd begun to make slow, methodical laps back and forth across the pool. "Since you posted a No Fishing sign and did the gorilla mating dance around her chair, I'm assuming that indifferent isn't the case, yet holding out doesn't seem particularly right, either. So what gives?"

"She's a friend," Hank told him tonelessly. "I'm just watching out for her." Jeez, what a self-serving lie.

"And that's it?"

Hank ignored Jamie's casual, searching look and drank his beer. He nodded, reluctant to admit the truth. "That's it."

Voicing the thoughts would, for reasons he didn't understand, make them all the more true. Final. Voice beget action and action was simply out of the question.

It would ruin everything. Their friendship would be over and he valued that relationship too much to jeopardize it with something as fleeting as sex. Even great sex.

Jamie arched a brow. "So as far as you're concerned, she's fair game?"

Hank's fingers inexplicably cramped around his longneck. "No," he said tightly. "If she was fair game, then I wouldn't have come over here and ran everyone off. She's not fair game. She's *no* kind of game. She's a friend looking for trouble, and I intend to keep her out of it.''

Jamie tipped his head back knowingly and an annoying smile turned his lips. ''Ah, so you're protecting her from herself?'' He nodded, the sarcastic bastard. ''Very noble.''

Hank expelled a mighty breath and gestured irritably. ''Look, she came down here with enough rubbers to outfit the Tennessee Titans for several months and a bunch of how-to sex magazines. She's trolling, just looking to get laid. I don't—''

A bark of dry laughter erupted from Jamie's throat. ''And that's supposed to be discouraging?''

Hank developed an eye twitch. ''It's out of character, not Samantha's style.''

Jamie shrugged. ''Maybe she's changed her style.''

Hank frowned. That disturbing thought had occurred to him as well. Still, no matter how many outward changes she made to herself, she couldn't change who she was on the inside, couldn't change her character. Hank slowly shook his head. ''No, that's not it. She's rooming with me—Tina screwed up again,'' he said, exasperated. ''But at least this time it was in my favor.''

Jamie chuckled. ''I'll say.''

Hank swore. ''What I meant was I'll be able to keep an eye on her,'' he said through gritted teeth.

''A real hardship.''

Hank cut him a look. "Asshole."

Jamie laughed and his smile faded. "She's an adult, Hank. Personally, I think you should offer advice and butt out. She won't appreciate your interference."

"Not now, maybe. But later she will."

Jamie shot him a skeptical glance. "I wouldn't be so sure."

"Look, I know Samantha," Hank insisted, growing less confident of himself as their conversation progressed. "She's not cut out for what she's looking for. She's too…nice."

"She seems very nice," Jamie agreed. "And she's *very* hot. If she sets her mind to it, you won't be able to stop her." Their gazes slid to Samantha once more. She'd flipped over, and was now doing a slow, lazy backstroke that pushed her new, bigger breasts up and out of the water in a very lust-provoking fashion. Heat stirred in his loins. "She could have had any guy at the table today simply by crooking her little finger."

Did he think he didn't know that? Hank thought angrily, not appreciating the reminder. He'd known it, dammit, that's why he'd run them all off. He had to unlock his jaw in order to respond. "I'll handle it."

And he would, or die trying. She would go back to Colorado in the same state she arrived in, by

God, with all of her extra-large condoms accounted
for. He took another draw from his beer.

"So you're not interested?" Jamie asked in a
deceptively casual voice.

Hank tensed, shook his head. "It's not like that,"
he lied.

"You're sure?"

He nodded, couldn't push the fib past his lips.

Jamie smiled and something about that lazy
checkmate grin made Hank's chest fill with dread.
"Then you won't mind if I invite her to dinner,
then."

Before Hank could form a protest, Jamie stood,
flashed him a wolfish grin—one that would ultimately cost him his teeth, Hank abruptly decided—
and dove into the pool.

A litany of curses streamed through his head and
seconds later, Hank, too, was cutting through the
water.

Not no, but hell no.

He had dinner plans for Samantha—they needed
to catch up on old times, dammit—and he wasn't
about to let his so-called friend screw him out of
the chance, the opportunistic bastard. He wanted to
take her to dinner—he always did when she came
down, Hank thought, perturbed. Come to think of
it, her vacation was usually spent with him. Not just
at his B&B, but *with him.* They inevitably shared
their meals, caught a movie, went beach-combing,

swimming and sailing. She'd even occasionally helped him out when the need arose.

When the need arose...

Sweet Lord, that was it, Hank thought as sudden inspiration stuck. He'd been going about this all wrong, he realized as a plan slowly unfolded in his tortured, panic-ridden brain. He knew exactly how to keep her so occupied that he wouldn't have to worry about her finding a lover—she wouldn't have the time, nor the energy. Hank grinned.

He'd put her new-and-improved ass to work.

5

SAMANTHA REGRETTED HAVING to decline Jamie's
dinner invitation, but before she could continue
with her plans for the week she needed to take care
of one little thing first—Hank.

She popped an antihistamine into her mouth and
chased it with a sip of soda, then shoved her feet
into her sandals and checked her reflection in the
mirror once more before leaving the room. Hank
had had some last-minute business to take care of,
so they'd agreed to meet on the front porch.

Samantha made her way outside, then sat down
and toed the old white wicker swing into motion.
The salty breeze lifted the hair away from her face,
bringing a smile to her lips. She loved the smell,
the very flavor of the air here. Screeching seagulls
dove in and out of the surf and the sound combined
with the rhythmic crash of the waves was music to
her ears.

This was her favorite part of the day, when time
seemed to hold its breath in awe of creation. The
beach was essentially deserted, only true sea-lovers
like herself outside to appreciate it. The sky was a

mixture of pale blues, pinks, lavenders and oranges and the sun melted against the horizon like a giant scoop of ice cream. Samantha sucked in a deep breath and savored every sensation, every detail, let her eyes drift shut as she took it all in.

It tasted like…home.

God, she couldn't wait to get back here, couldn't wait to have her own little stretch of beach. For years anytime she'd thought of home, curiously the house she'd shared with her grandmother, or even the one she'd shared with her parents, hadn't been what her memory had called to mind—it was this house. The big, old Victorian style home was absolutely beautiful.

White with green shutters and decorated with wraparound porches, soaring turrets, hand-carved finials and scalloped siding, the house looked whimsical against the backdrop of the sea, almost magical. The eaves dripped miles of fancy fretwork and an old weather vane stood proudly on the roof of a small cupola.

Samantha had spent years fantasizing about living in this house with Hank, filling it with happy, noisy children. Particularly after her parents had died. But as time had worn on, she'd realized the futility of the wish and had finally had to abandon that dream. For reasons she didn't understand, she'd never been able to picture herself anywhere but here, couldn't imagine having a family with anyone but Hank. Her dream children always had white-blond hair and sea-blue eyes, little chubby-cheeked miniatures of Hank. She supposed that someday another guy would come along that she might fall in love with, but she grimly doubted it.

Hank Masterson had had her heart since she was five years old and she didn't ever anticipate getting it back to give to someone else.

It was a sad realization, but one that she'd accepted. Samantha blew out a sigh. The best that she could hope for was to move home closer to him and maintain their friendship. She didn't just miss Orange Beach—she missed Hank, and the two were hopelessly intertwined in her memory.

Though she'd barely missed the registration cutoff, she'd turned in her *Belle of the Beach* form, along with the twenty-dollar registration fee. It was a minimal investment for the potential reward. She didn't necessarily think she'd win, but she was just optimistic enough to try. According to the form, secret judges would be milling around throughout the week, the Fried Chicken and Iced Tea cook-off—which she still thought was ludicrous—would be held on Saturday afternoon. The official pageant would be Saturday night. She was essentially blowing an entire day of her vacation on it, but the idea of being able to move home made it worth the risk. Like he'd said, what did she have to lose?

Hank was undoubtedly laboring under the incorrect assumption that his poor, pitiful me display in the pool this afternoon, combined with the threatening way he'd glared at Jamie was the reason she'd opted to go to dinner with him instead of Jamie.

He thought wrong.

Yes, they traditionally had dinner together her first night back—as well as every other meal—and yes, the majority of her vacation was spent with the two of them playing catch-up—something she knew she would miss terribly—but she couldn't very well find a lover—her consolation prize for never having him—if she were hanging around Hank all the time, and she certainly wouldn't be able to find one if he kept running off every potential guy. Irritation vibrated her nerves and her womb issued a long, pitiful howl of neglect. Furthermore, she only had a small window of opportunity here to work with. This was the perfect time to throw caution to the wind and take a lover.

Jamie, thank God, seemed to find Hank's blustering behavior only mildly amusing, and didn't appear to be the least bit put off, yet—in fact, though Hank didn't know it, they'd decided to meet for drinks after dinner—but Samantha couldn't count on that particular attitude to continue. The simplest thing to do was have a much-needed chat with Hank and make him back off.

The jealous boyfriend act—when she knew he

didn't have any such feelings—was going to have to stop.

Aside from being unequivocally, provokingly annoying given the pains she'd gone to in order to plan this week, it was also unexpectedly painful. A curious knot formed in her throat. It made her think of what might have been, what she wished for but knew she'd never have—him.

She'd resigned herself to that end long ago, but her foolish heart, she supposed, would never truly stop hoping. Unfortunately her heart and her brain weren't in agreement. While her heart wished to hope, her brain told her the futility of that emotion and longed to channel that energy to a more productive—attainable—goal.

Like having a much-needed rite-of-passage orgasm.

If Hank continued to circle her and paw the ground like a snorting bull, she didn't have a prayer of finding a guy, then achieving her goal. Every sexual feminine part of her cried out in rebellion of that thought. An achy, itchy sort of heat rolled through her body, concentrated in her nipples and her womb, making her squirm with sexual frustration. Her body hungered for release, craved that intimate physical contact she'd never had. She couldn't wait any longer, she simply couldn't, Samantha thought suppressing a silent wail.

She *wanted*.

Her sex diet, the ultimate secret weapon for the unremarkable, was definitely working. In fact, were she not allergic to the seafood, she would undoubtedly keep it up permanently. Not only did she seem to be emitting enough pheromones to attract every guy in a ten-mile radius, the diet had the unexpected bonus of making her feel beautiful, confident and desirable. She *felt* sexy, a singularly wonderful sensation, particularly since she'd never felt that way before.

It also sharpened the edge of her need, which quite honestly had been lethal before she went on the diet. If she got any more horny—any more desperate—she was liable to skip the preliminaries, snag the next guy she saw and drag him off to have her wicked way with him.

Ironically Hank chose that exact moment to walk out the door.

Samantha ducked her head and chuckled under her breath.

"What's so funny?" he asked. Looking more handsome than any man had a right to be, he strolled over to the swing and sat down beside her. Samantha sneaked a covert glance at his profile, traced the angular planes of his achingly familiar face, let her gaze linger on that sexy, perpetually smiling wicked-looking mouth. His smell, a seductive combination of beach, male and a cool, clean cologne wafted around her. He'd changed out of his customary trunks and dressed in a pale yellow linen shirt and comfortable white cargo shorts. A pair of leather sandals rounded out the casual outfit and everything about him exuded sexy, effortless confidence.

Would that it could be so simple for her, Samantha thought enviously. She'd changed her entire appearance, had gone on a sex diet, for pity's sake, all for one week out of thousands in her life to have what he took for granted—sex appeal—and she knew that the moment she went off the diet, her tiny run in the hot department would be over. Finis.

Which was all the more reason why she had to make this week work.

"Nothing's wrong," Samantha told him, feeling her heart rate jump into overdrive at his nearness. God, did he have to be so gorgeous? Those heavy-lidded clear blue eyes were startlingly beautiful set beneath his pale brows. "I was just appreciating a little irony."

He arched a brow. "Oh? How's that?"

She gave her head a small shake. "It was nothing. Are you about ready?"

Hank pulled in a deep breath, savoring the late-afternoon breeze as she had, then released it with a long whoosh. His arm brushed hers, sending little sparklers of heat dancing up her arm. "Yeah, I'm starved. How about Lambert's?"

Samantha inwardly winced. She'd like nothing

better than a trip to Lambert's—the café served true southern fare and had the distinct reputation for throwing rolls to patrons rather than simply handing them out. Her trip was never complete until she'd had a hot yeast roll hurled at her from across the room, or a helping of their legendary pass-around's, but regrettably, it would have to be a tradition they forewent this go 'round. Samantha suppressed a sigh. Her diet had to be followed to the letter, and unfortunately fried okra, pinto beans, and sorghum molasses weren't a part of it. She'd be having seafood for dinner and some sort of chocolate dessert.

In addition to containing components which helped stimulate the transmission and conduction of nerve impulses, chocolate was also an organoleptic food, or a food in which the sensual texture, color and scent helped put a person in the mood. As far as that part of it went, Samantha was there—she couldn't get any more in the mood. Still, it was part of the diet and she didn't dare take the chance of going off it for even one meal. She exhaled a small breath. Tonight oysters were on the menu.

Samantha winced and shook her head. "Er... I was kind of hoping we could head over to Captain Jack's."

His brow folded in perplexity. "The oyster bar?"

"Yep."

Looking somewhat bemused, Hank nodded amiably. "Er...sure, we can do that."

Obviously he hadn't remembered her seafood allergy and she wondered how much longer it would be before that little memory surfaced. She'd readied an explanation. Still...

Hank nudged the swing to a halt, then unfolded his six-foot frame from the seat and offered her a hand up. His calloused palm connected with hers and the simple contact made her entire body warm and tingly, made her blood sing in her veins. Not good, Samantha thought. Pre-diet, that tingly sensation would have only extended to her shoulder. Presently, her entire body sang like a tuning fork. Jamie had helped her out of the pool this afternoon and she'd barely felt a vibe in her palm, nothing compared to the sexual energy Hank instilled with a mere brush of his fingers.

Samantha refused to consider the negative implications of that thought and gave herself a mental kick for even allowing herself to compare the two. She couldn't have Hank, dammit, so there was nothing to compare.

Hank was off-limits.

But she could have someone else—deserved someone else—possibly Jamie, which was the reason for this dinner in the first place, Samantha thought, preparing herself for the hour ahead. She dreaded the coming conversation with Hank—knew he'd undoubtedly blow a gasket when she essentially told him her plan. She had no intention of telling him about the sex diet—he'd think it was foolish, she knew—but their relationship had always been based on honesty, on trust, and she'd decided to come clean about her quest for an orgasm.

Given his recent reactions to the idea of her having sex, having sexual thoughts, etc…Sam had decided that a little plain-speaking was in order. Whether he realized it or not, she *didn't* have a Y chromosome—she was a woman, one that had needs. He could like it or lump it. A grin rolled around her lips. She had a feeling a little *lumping* would be in order.

Regardless, the ultimate decision was hers and she'd put too much time and effort into having this week for herself to let his head-in-the-sand mentality stop her. One way or another, his blinders were coming off.

Shuck me, suck me, eat me raw.

She'd just had to buy the damned T-shirt, Hank thought in miserable frustration as he imagined her doing those very things to him. Quite graphically. It wasn't enough that she'd sat there beneath a sign emblazoned with the same sexually provocative slogan all through their dinner—that he'd watched her savor each and every bite of her oyster platter—now he had to endure this as well.

Not only had she brought the T-shirt, she'd gone

into the bathroom and put it on. Hank's fingers twitched with irritation and longing. Now, *shuck me, suck me, eat me raw* was written across her new delectable breasts and it was sheer hell, because that's precisely what he'd like to do to her. What he'd wanted to do to her for years.

Keeping the attraction in check had been a monumental undertaking as it was, but over the years he'd learned to deal with it. He'd had to, otherwise he'd have gone insane. Initially he'd remained in Tuscaloosa, rather than returning to Orange Beach. It had been hard at first, but under the circumstances, he'd felt like the decision had been the right one. Then Sam had moved to Aspen, which had given him the opportunity to really get his head together. Since then, the buzz of awareness had been his constant companion—anytime he thought of her, talked to her, or saw her—but he'd always been able to keep it in check, had always remained in control.

But he grimly suspected that wouldn't be the case anymore. Be it her new breasts, or her quest for sex, or simply the end of his rope, he didn't know. He only knew that he couldn't let her shag a guy right under his nose—hell, most likely under his roof. It was blasphemous.

Hank needed her to be his friend more than he needed her to be his lover—that's why he'd put a stop to that near kiss. That's why he'd never tipped his hand. Lovers were a dime a dozen, but a true friend was rare. He knew that, and yet he was suddenly hit with the inexplicable urge to be both to her.

Which was out of the question.

His gaze slid to Samantha who walked silently beside him and something peculiar, not altogether unpleasant, moved through his chest. Would that things could be different, Hank thought. That she wanted him as well. There used to be a time when he suspected that, like him, her feelings were more than platonic, but if that was the case, he hadn't seen a glimmer of the sentiment in years. She seemed completely happy with the status quo, had never done anything to make him think otherwise. And her showing up here, packing condoms like a traveling salesmen definitely didn't inspire any reason to suggest otherwise.

Still, he would have thought that over the years she would have found a guy, would have settled down with a dependable husband and a passel of kids. He'd been expecting the call, but it had never come. Why? Hank wondered now. Were men blind in Aspen? Was she too picky? It didn't make any sense.

As for himself, Hank knew the reason he hadn't found someone else—Sam. He could blame it on not having enough time to put into a relationship, or not willing to invest emotionally, but the bottom line was he knew no other woman would do, and any other woman would be a substitute for the real thing. Furthermore, that substitute wouldn't permit the sort of friendship he and Sam shared, and he'd rather have that friendship and a string of faceless lovers than a poor man's Sam.

Captain Jack's Oyster Bar was located on a gorgeous stretch of sand just east of Ono Island. A light-lined boardwalk meandered down to near shore and, though it was almost seven o'clock, day still edged out night in a beautiful display of purple and orange color. Music from the bar wafted with her fruity scent, creating a curiously intimate haze around his head. God, she smelled fantastic, Hank thought. Tantalizing.

They'd decided to take a stroll before returning to Clearwater and Hank was glad. He'd laid his "poor, tired, overworked me" trap and was simply waiting for her to walk into it. As far as a plan went, it wasn't the best, but anything was better than the alternative.

Conversation over dinner had moved smoothly, like it always did. They'd talked about movies they'd seen, ones they'd like to see as well as current events and mutual acquaintances. Hank had sprinkled in enough complaints about being tired, overworked and understaffed to pave the way to ask Samantha to help out. He hated that it had come to this—that he'd have to essentially wreck her vacation to save his sanity—but it couldn't be helped.

At the end of the boardwalk, Samantha slid out of her shoes, then stepped into the sand and curled her toes. "Ah," she sighed with a smile. "Heaven."

Hank grinned, poked his tongue in his cheek. "Doesn't take much to please you, does it?"

Her lips curled into an endearing smile and another bolt of heat zapped his groin. "Pathetic, isn't it?"

"Nah, it just means you're happier than most people."

She mulled that over for a minute, then gave him a curious look, as though he'd uttered some profound statement. "You're right. I am. Come on," she told him. "Let's get our feet wet."

Hank followed her down the surf. A wave licked at her feet and he watched another silent sigh slip past her lips. The wind played with her long strawberry-blond curls, alternately sweeping it away from her face, then sending it swishing across her cheeks. She curled her toes into the sand once more. "Now, this is what I miss the most about coming here."

"What? Not me?" Hank asked, mockingly wounded.

Something dark flickered in her gaze, but she covered it with a laugh so quickly that Hank was inclined to believe he'd imagined it. "Ah. Does your ego need stroking, poor baby?" she teased.

His ego was fine, but he could think of something else that could use a little stroking, Hank thought, imagining her small capable hands wrapped around his rod. He mentally swore. "Go ahead and make fun," he told her, essaying a laugh. "You know I miss you when you're gone."

She shot him a probing look. "And just how am I supposed to know that?"

"Because I've told you."

She chuckled and sidled farther down the beach. "Er…no you haven't," she said matter-of-factly.

He hadn't? Hank wondered, taken aback. "Well," he hedged uncomfortably. "It's understood."

She laughed again, the sound hearty and melodious. "Translation: Guy Speak for 'you're underappreciated and I should have told you.' Or, 'I meant to tell you, but I didn't because I'm a thoughtless man.'"

Did she honestly not realize how much he cared for her? How much he valued her friendship? If so, that would be rectified before she went back to Colorado. In fact, he'd start now. "Thoughtless behavior duly noted," he told her, forcing a lighter note into his voice. "And for the record, I miss you when you're gone." He blew out a breath, shoved his hands into his pockets, kicked at a nonexistent rock at his feet. "With Mom and Dad in Alaska, it feels more like home when you're here."

"Thanks," she murmured softly. "Clearwater feels like home." She paused and her twinkling gaze tangled with his. "I'm planning on moving back here, you know."

Unexpected delight settled in his chest. "You are? When?"

She bent over and picked up a shell, inspected it before slipping it into her pocket. "As soon as I can save up enough money for a down payment for my own little piece of sand." She shrugged lightly. "I've been stashing a little here and a little there, but I'm still several thousand away." She cast him a sardonic glance and poked her tongue in her cheek. "Of course, I could always win that *Belle of the Beach* contest, and be back before Halloween."

"It's not out the realm of possibility, you know," Hank told her. And it sounded absolutely perfect, he thought, unreasonably pleased. Having Samantha back in Orange Beach would be fantastic. No more solo evenings spent at home during the off-season—she'd be there to share them with him. And during the busy season, she could help him. Hell, she knew as much about running his business as he did, Hank thought as the idea gained momentum. In fact, he'd implemented several of her ideas. The cabana bar and grill out by the pool had been her brainchild. She had a real knack for making people feel at home, for making them feel special. She would be a true asset to his business.

Samantha snorted indelicately, bent over and splashed water up over her legs. "Yeah, right."

"You do," Hank insisted. "You're gorgeous."

She stilled, seemingly startled, then briskly straightened and managed a shaky laugh. "Well, thanks. It means a lot coming from you."

Hank frowned over the "coming from you" comment. It should have felt like a compliment...but for some reason it didn't. "What do you mean *coming from me?*"

She gave him an adorably droll smile. "Because we both know how ugly I was."

"You were not ugly," Hank denied automatically.

She shot him a pointed look. "Please."

His cheeks flushed and he shoved his hands into his pockets once more. "You were...awkward at times, but never ugly." She hadn't been ugly. Not to him, anyway.

"Thank you. That's a very charitable description."

"I'm not being charitable, smart ass," Hank insisted, mildly annoyed. "I'm being honest. You were not ugly."

"Whatever." Her eyes twinkled. "It hardly matters now, seeing how gorgeous I am."

"That's right." He shot her a look, hesitated. That was the opening he'd been waiting for. "Speaking of which, there's something I've been wanting to talk to you about. I—"

"Oh, me, too," she interrupted, and waved her hand airily. "But you go first."

Hank grimaced. What did she want to talk to him about? he wondered, then forced the thought from his mind. He needed to focus here. There was a fine line between delicate and direct. He had to walk it carefully, otherwise he'd piss her off.

Hank rubbed the back of his neck, cast her a look and charged ahead. "Look, Sam, I don't know whether you realize it or not…but you're sending out a vibe." He knew perfectly well that she knew it, he'd just needed some way to broach the subject.

Hank detected a slight quiver in her bottom lip before she sank her teeth into it. She blinked innocently. "Oh? And what sort of vibe would that be?"

"A come-pump-me vibe," he said, annoyed.

"Good," she told him, rocking back on her heels in obvious delight. That wicked glint he noticed earlier gleamed particularly bright. "That's precisely the kind of vibe I've been hoping to send out."

Hank pulled in a deep breath through his nostrils in a vain attempt to stay calm. So it was as he'd suspected. She was looking for a lover—and she wasn't looking at him.

A dull throb commenced at the base of his skull. "What do you mean, good?"

"Precisely what I said. Good."

"Why is it good?" Hank asked and resisted the urge to grind his teeth.

She cast him a sidelong glance. "I would have thought the condoms in my bag would have tipped you off."

"Cute, but humor me," Hank replied tightly.

"Fine. It's good," she said patiently, "because in order to get what I want, that's exactly the type of vibe I need to send out."

The throb bisected his skull and settled between his eyes. "And what exactly is it that you want?" He had to push the words from his cottony mouth. He knew what she wanted, but for some wholly sadistic reason, he wanted to hear her say it.

She winced. "You're not going to like it, Hank. But I'm glad that you asked because it makes it easier for me to tell you." Her eyes narrowed. "Because after I tell you, I expect you to butt out."

"Then tell me."

She shrugged lightly and an evil little gleam danced in her pale green eyes. "Fine. I want an orgasm."

6

HE SWALLOWED. REPEATEDLY. "An orgasm?"

Sam nodded succinctly. "An orgasm."

He squeezed his eyes tightly shut.

"Is this what you needed to talk to me about?"

Samantha inclined her head. "It plays a significant part, yes."

"How so?"

Samantha hesitated. So far, so good. But now came the tricky part. She'd been fully prepared to lay into him over being such an obnoxious ass out by the pool, but her ire had ebbed through dinner and had fled completely when he'd glibly announced that she was gorgeous. Samantha swallowed tightly. No one had ever told her she was pretty, or attractive, not even her parents. She'd always been *such a sweet girl* or *such a nice girl*. Never beautiful, or pretty or even cute, for that matter.

Hank—whose opinion she valued above all others—had called her gorgeous as though it were simply a given, had said it as casually as one might say, the sky is blue, or water is wet. Her heart had all but stopped and her chest tightened until she could barely draw a breath. She'd played it off, but she'd been quaking inside.

Samantha would have thought that sharing her sexual inexperience would be heartily embarrassing, however, now that the time had come, the sensation she felt was more akin to relief. She'd made some good friends over the years in Aspen, one in particular she could comfortably bare her soul to.

But, whether he knew it or not, Hank had always been her best friend, and getting this off her chest didn't feel bizarre at all—it felt natural. Furthermore, God knows he'd never held back. Her lips curled with painful humor. He'd shared intimate details of his early sex life with her over the years. She'd pasted a smile on her face and listened, while inwardly her heart had been breaking.

That had been uncomfortable.

Hank didn't want to think about her having sex or having an orgasm because he looked at her and she imagined he saw a little sister, not a person he was in love with. Well, he could just suck it up. This was part of being a friend. She'd been a good friend to him. He could damn well reciprocate the gesture.

Samantha blew out a breath, absently buried her big toe in the sand. "Look, Hank, the long and short of it is...I've never had an orgasm. And I want one, dammit. It's time."

Looking equally astounded and uncomfortable, he cleared his throat. "You've, uh, never…"

"Had sex?" Samantha supplied helpfully.

He paled.

"Yes," she told him with exaggerated patience. Honestly. "I've had sex. Once, many years ago."

His eyes widened. "But you never mentioned…you never said anything."

A droll smile curled her lips and she rolled her eyes. "Trust me, it didn't bear mentioning. It was an unremarkable experience. I deserve better," Samantha said matter-of-factly, "and I fully intend to have better. This week." Samantha crossed her arms over her chest, ignored a prickle of irritation. "And I can't do that if you're running off every potential guy." She softened her voice and laid a hand on his arm. "I know that you're only looking out for me—you always have and I appreciate it— but I'm a big girl, Hank, and I've put a lot of effort into making myself attractive, making myself…desirable." She huffed an exasperated breath, considered the truth of that statement. "Trust me, it's not been easy. But, the effort seems to be paying off. I had a nice little cache of guys around me this afternoon—" her eyes narrowed "—until you came along and blew it. I'm asking you, as my friend, to cease and desist with the guerilla warfare tactics. I don't have time for it and I know what I'm doing."

Hank grimly shook his head. "I don't think you do."

"And you're certainly entitled to your opinion," she replied levelly. "However the ultimate decision is mine and I think that I do."

Hank blew out a frustrated breath, gestured wildly. His antics sent a throng of nearby seagulls squawking into the air. "So you're just going to randomly pick a guy? Just snag one out of the crowd and have sex with him? Is that it?"

Samantha nodded. "That's the general plan."

"Well, that's ignorant."

She blinked, taken aback. "I'm sorry?"

"Undoubtedly you will be," Hank said with an annoying snort of derision.

"Hank," Samantha warned, exasperated. "Just what the hell is the problem? What do you do when you want to get laid?"

His mouth opened, then closed. Opened again. "Well, I—"

"You find someone to seduce, that's what you do," Samantha supplied knowingly. "Why should it be any different for me? Why is it ignorant for me to do what I know you've done repeatedly?"

He exhaled mightily, began to pace the wet sand back and forth in front of her. "Because I'm *me* and you're you and…and it's just not safe."

Samantha nodded succinctly. "That's why I brought the condoms."

He stopped and glared at her and the sinking sun backlit him in a gorgeous display of orange, making him look like an avenging sea god. "It's still not safe, dammit."

She crossed her arms over her chest and rolled her eyes. "Yeah, well, being an orgasm virgin at twenty-six isn't safe, either—safe for my mental health. I need— I want—" Samantha whimpered, groaned, threw her head back and emitted a frustrated growl low in her throat. "How do I make you understand?"

Hank rubbed the back of his flushed neck, swallowed awkwardly. "It's not that I don't understand. Clearly—" he shot her a pained look "—you're horny. I know what it's like to be horny." He looked heavenward and heaved a long-suffering sigh. "But there are…other ways of relieving sexual frustration than taking a lover," he said haltingly, clearly desperate to change her mind.

Samantha quirked a brow. "If you're suggesting that I masturbate, then you can save your breath. I don't want to masturbate," she said stubbornly. "I want to have sex. With a man. And have an orgasm."

She heard his teeth grind. "So you've said."

"And I can't do that if you keep sabotaging me. Enough already, Hank. Back off. Understood?"

Hank finally nodded, blew out a breath. "So what does this mean? For the rest of the week you're going to be trolling for a guy? You're not going to have time for me?''

Samantha gently shook her head, winced when a thorn of regret pricked her heart. "Not as much as I normally do, no. I need to do this, Hank. I want to know what the big deal is. I didn't get anything out of the first time—nothing." Samantha laughed darkly, shook her head. "It was horrible. Is it so awful that I want to know what good sex feels like? Is that so hard for you to understand?"

"No, that's not hard to understand." His voice had developed a dry rasp. "But why did you have to do it here? Why now?" he asked suspiciously. "There's more to this than you're telling me, isn't there?"

"No," Samantha lied, feeling the telltale heat of guilt climb her neck. Did he have to be so damned perceptive? God, he knew her too well. If he was having this much trouble accepting the fact that she wanted to get laid, he'd be truly horrified at the lengths she'd gone to. There was no way in hell she planned to tell him about the sex diet. He'd have a stroke.

To Samantha's immeasurable disquiet, he continued to study her intensely. "Furthermore, how are we supposed to get you prepped for this contest— and I *know* you can win—if you're out combing the beaches for a man-whore?" He scowled. "I thought you said you wanted to move back here."

Though she took exception to the man-whore comment, Samantha bit her tongue and refrained from scorching his ears with a few hot expletives. "I do want to move back here," she insisted. "We'll still have time. Honestly, Hank. All I have to do is fry a chicken. It's not rocket science."

He tsked skeptically. "Whatever you think."

Okay, enough of this, Samantha decided. A subject change was in order. "What was it you wanted to ask me about?"

He gave her a blank look.

"A few minutes ago," she reminded him. "You said you wanted to ask me about something. What was it?"

Those pale brows winged up his tanned forehead and he eventually murmured a knowing, "Oh."

"Oh...what?"

Hank shook his head. "Forget it. It's a moot point now."

What was a moot point? Samantha wondered, intrigued. "What?" she repeated.

"Really, forget it," Hank insisted mysteriously. He gave his head a small shake, and another humorless smile edged up the corner of his lips. "I couldn't ask you now, anyway."

"Ask me what?"

"Really, Samantha, forget it." He grunted, laughed without humor. "You won't have the time."

Samantha blew out a disgusted breath. "Oh, for pity's sake, Hank," she said, thoroughly exasperated. "I won't have the time for what?"

He shot her a sheepish look. "To help me."

She frowned. "Help you? Help you do what?"

"Around the B&B." He sighed wearily, pushed a hand through his hair. "Things are really hectic right now, and you've seen firsthand how well Tina can handle the front desk. I'm beat, can't get caught up and, short of a clone, I'm not going to be able to." He blew out a dejected breath. "Like I said, forget it. I'll figure something out."

So that's what all those little leading comments about him being worn-out and understaffed were about, Samantha realized with a belated start. He'd been fishing for an offer from her, and she'd been so concerned with her orgasm-quest that she hadn't caught on.

Samantha gazed at his woebegone expression and, though she firmly believed he'd manufactured it in order to manipulate her into helping him, she nonetheless couldn't argue with the fine lines of fatigue etched around his mouth and eyes. He was right. She *had* seen how busy he'd been, how inept Tina was, and could tell by his face he was genuinely stressed. Genuinely tired. In addition, she knew he wouldn't ask her to help him unless he truly needed it. She couldn't in good conscience refuse, not when he'd been such a good friend to her.

"I can help," Samantha said consideringly. She absently chewed her bottom lip and mulled it over. In fact, rather than keep looking for a guy, maybe she should just settle on the one Hank *hadn't* managed to run off this afternoon. That would certainly speed up the process and it's not like she'd had a huge window of opportunity to deal with, anyway. If she simply set her sights on Jamie—her lead contender—then the time she'd spend looking for other guys could be spent helping out Hank. She'd get her orgasm and he'd get his help. Seemed like a workable plan.

Hank's lips curled into a droll smile, though traces of his irritation still lingered in the tense muscles of his face. "Won't that cut into your trolling time?" he asked with a sardonic arch of his brow.

Samantha made up her mind, thoughtfully tapped her chin. "Actually, no."

Confusion wrinkled his brow. "No?"

"I'm through trolling for guys—"

Hank breathed a deep sigh of relief. "Thank God. I knew you'd come to your—"

"—because I've already found one."

Hank's head whipped around. "What? When? Who?" His frown grew more comically pronounced as he fired the questions at her.

Samantha turned and started back across the

beach toward the boardwalk. A sand crab scuttled out of her path. "Add a 'where' and we're back in English 101," she said drolly, purposely ignoring his questions. "Come on, Hank. You can tell me what you want me to do on the way back to Clearwater. I've got a date."

"What?"

Now that she'd firmed up her plan, she was ready to put it into action. She dusted off her feet and slid them back into her sandals. When she thought about it, Hank asking her for help might have been a blessing in disguise. She might have wasted the majority of her week trying to scope out her options. "I'm meeting someone for a drink and I need to get back."

And they really needed to get a move on, particularly since Hank would most likely keep her busy all day tomorrow. That would be fine...provided her nights were free. A thrill whipped through her.

"Who?" Hank demanded ominously, hot on her heels. "Who are you meeting for a drink?"

"Jamie," Sam told him. She whirled around to face him, forcing Hank to draw up short. She determinedly ignored the prickle of awareness that tripped up her spine. "And I'm going alone. Which means, just for clarification purposes, *without you.* No more funny business, Hank. You have to butt out."

"But—"

''But nothing. I'm getting laid this week,'' she all but growled, ''whether you like it or not.''

Hank's miserably thunderous expression left little doubt as to which category he'd fall into.

HOURS LATER HANK MILLED AROUND the bedroom and impatiently waited for Samantha to return. The moment she made it back, Hank fully intended to go and, if necessary, drag Jamie out of bed and beat the living hell out of him. His jaw ached from clenching it so hard. Obviously he hadn't made himself clear to his *former* friend when he'd told him that Samantha was ''off-limits.'' Since verbal communication had failed, he'd resort to physical communication, ensuring that Jamie couldn't possibly mistake Hank's meaning again.

He glanced at the clock and felt his blood pressure boil to stroke level. She'd been gone for two hours.

Two hours.

A lot could happen—repeatedly, Hank knew—in one hundred and twenty minutes and, presently his sadistic mind had decided to torture him with horribly graphic scenarios. The idea of simply going by the bar and spying on them was almost overpowering, but Hank checked the impulse. Samantha would never forgive him if he interfered. He knew it and yet...

Jesus.

Hank plopped down on the sofa and his breath left him in a long, dejected whoosh. For all intents and purposes, he'd felt the ground shift beneath his feet when she'd told him she wanted an orgasm. He'd known the moment he'd found those condoms what her intentions were, had never doubted for a moment that she'd planned to take a lover this week. But listening to her tell him that she wanted an orgasm... Now that had simply been sheer hell.

Then, when she'd proceeded to tell him about her one and only suck-ass lover who'd been given the ultimate prize—her virginity—and the sorry little bastard had failed to give her even the slightest amount of pleasure, Hank had been hit with the combined urge to a.) rectify that injustice at once, preferably at that precise moment with his tongue, and b.) hunt the little bastard down and introduce his fist to the guy's unworthy, ungrateful face.

Regrettably, neither one of those stress-relieving options were readily available and, as a result, he was about as wired, annoyed, thwarted and irritated as a man could get.

Hank cracked his knuckles. Luckily Jamie had pissed him off and he'd be able to vent a little of his frustration on him.

But as he'd alternately paced and sat, fumed and stewed, the one thing that had become glaringly obvious to him was the fact that he'd obviously made a huge mistake all those years ago. He should have kissed her then, that first time he'd been hit with the urge on the ferry. Or better still, he should have followed through with that near-kiss later that summer. If he had, then none of this would be happening. She'd never have squandered her virginity on some uninspired ass, and he could have made absolutely certain that she'd been satisfied. In fact, he'd happily spend the rest of his life giving her as many orgasms as she could possibly handle.

Though he'd grown increasingly uncomfortable throughout her little I-want-an-orgasm soliloquy, Hank had listened to her and the irony of what she was telling him had all but whacked him between the eyes.

Or in the groin, as the case may be.

The entire time that she'd been standing there, telling him about how desperately she needed to get laid, how much she wanted to know what the big deal was about sex and the Big O, Hank's dick had speedily risen to the occasion and he would have gladly lowered her to the sand and granted her that very wish. With his hands, his tongue, his rod. Whatever. He just wanted to taste her. Wanted to be the one to see her to that special place. He didn't want anyone else to touch her, didn't want anyone else giving her the orgasm she wanted.

He wanted to do it.

He wanted to be the one to give it to her.

For one insane instant, he'd almost told her that,

too. Had nearly lost himself completely in the stress and the attraction and had almost begged her for the chance.

But the caution he'd exercised over the last several years was a hard habit to break, and he'd held his tongue.

He wished now that he hadn't, because he'd never—*never*—wanted a woman as much as he wanted Samantha. Had never felt his palms itch, or this quivery heat presently curling through his abdomen. Had never had a perpetual, ceaseless hardon. Hank glanced at the tent at the front of his shorts and a futile bark of laughter erupted from his throat. His poor rod had been at full attention since he saw her back. Her *back*, for heaven's sake.

The physical symptoms were enough to deal with, but there were also other wholly alarming side effects. Like the fact that he couldn't look at her without wanting to kiss her. Couldn't look at her without imagining framing her woefully familiar face with his hands and touching his lips to hers. While Hank enjoyed kissing, to be quite honest, it wasn't his most favorite form of foreplay. Generally he considered it a means to an end, a prelude to the ultimate payoff.

But the idea of kissing Samantha and the jittery sentiment that accompanied the thought scared the living hell out of him.

He could claim that he'd never wanted to jeopardize their friendship all he wanted, but Hank knew there was another reason as well, one that lurked in emotional waters best left uncharted.

Hank blew out a breath, glanced at the clock once more and felt his scalp cramp and his eyes narrow. His gut roiled with dread and his left eye began to twitch. He didn't know how on earth he had let this happen, how on earth he'd let himself become such a damned basket case, but it had to stop.

Right now.

And the only way he knew to do that would put he and Samantha at cross-purposes...because it meant he'd have to stop her from finding another guy. The only way she'd get that damned orgasm on this trip would be if he finally snapped, lost his freaking mind and gave her one.

Which, he thought resignedly, was exactly what he intended to do.

Did he have misgivings? Without a doubt. Telling her how he felt would permanently alter their relationship, but the alternative was simply out of the question. He couldn't knowingly let her sleep with another man. If anyone was going to find heaven between her delectable thighs, then by God that man was going to be him. No one else. After all, he'd wanted her the longest.

Whether she knew it or not, Sam was his. She

always had been. And he looked forward to convincing her…one orgasm at a time.

But first he'd need to level the playing field, which meant another conversation with Jamie would be in order.

7

JESUS, WHAT A MESS, Sam thought tiredly. She'd
been working on Hank's reservation system for the
better part of the day, but so far had made very
little progress. Hank hadn't been kidding when he
said that Tina had screwed things up. She smoth-
ered a groan. It would undoubtedly take her the rest
of the week to get it sorted out and running properly
again.

Which was undoubtedly what he'd counted on,
the sneaky bastard. Yes, she could tell that he was
tired and admittedly Tina was inept, but this was
nothing more than busy work to keep her occupied.
She knew it as well as she knew her own name.
Hank had been by a couple of times today, had
tsked regretfully about the mess, but she'd seen that
secret little grin and known precisely what it
meant—he wanted to keep her occupied, so that she
wouldn't have time to snag a lover.

When she'd finally made it back to his room last
night, Hank had still been fully dressed and, by the
look of supreme irritation and curious resignation
on his face, he'd not been pleased that she'd spent

several hours with Jamie. He'd obviously ignored an important errand in lieu of monitoring her comings and goings, because the moment she walked back into the room, he'd taken one look at her, his nostrils had flared and he'd calmly stormed from the room.

She'd heard him come back in around an hour later and had feigned sleep. She'd had all the confrontation she could stand for one day and arguing had been a moot point—she was going to do what she wanted to do and Hank would simply have to get over it.

She and Jamie had had a fantastic time. He had a great sense of humor, was a wonderful conversationalist. Though he hadn't made a move on her, she'd sensed his interest and it pleased her right down to her little toes. She imagined he'd been waiting for some kind of sign from her and, though she'd been eager to give it to him, Samantha had found herself hesitating.

Hank, damn him, had made her doubt whether or not she was doing the right thing. He'd made her have second thoughts and had undermined her progress. Granted, Jamie didn't make her tummy tremble, didn't make her panties wet, and she didn't stare at his mouth and wonder what it would be like to kiss him. She didn't fantasize about having his hands roaming over her body or his mouth suckling at her breasts.

Annoyingly, those feelings seemed to be reserved only for Hank.

But there had been a little wriggle of desire when he'd walked her back to the bedroom and kissed her cheek. He had a nice mouth, very carnal. Maybe if she increased her sex-diet portions she could work up a little more interest.

Besides, Samantha had the sneaking suspicion that no matter how much time she invested in finding another guy for the week, it wouldn't make any difference. She wanted Hank and in the absence of not having him, she would simply have to settle for someone else. Her lips quirked. If Gorgeous Jamie didn't crank her tractor, she seriously doubted she'd be able to find someone else who would.

She'd lain there last night and listened to Hank shed his clothes down to his boxers, then heard him sigh and settle himself onto the couch. For reasons which escaped her, she'd gotten the oddest impression that he'd purposely taken his time, had purposely wanted to make her squirm. There'd been something different about the way he'd looked at her. Something almost predatory, but she'd chalked the notion up to wishful thinking. Still, just listening to him undress had been more arousing than anything in her admittedly limited experience.

Her thighs had quivered with longing and a deep,

achy throb had built between her legs. Her nipples had tightened into hard, sensitive peaks and her breathing had become so shallow it was hard to force air into her lungs. Every particle in her being begged for release, begged to know what that sensation felt like.

Samantha had seen every inch of Hank's body at one point or another over the years and her sadistic memory had called his perfectly proportioned image immediately to the forefront of her mind. Broad, broad shoulders. Tanned, smooth skin over hard muscle. That pale sprinkling of crisp male hair that formed an inverted triangle on his splendidly sculpted chest, arrowed down and neatly bisected those six-pack abs, then disappeared beneath the waist band of his shorts. Long, muscular legs. She'd pulled the total package into focus, had imagined those heavy-lidded sea-blue eyes and that oh-so-wicked slow smile, and it had been all she could do not to scream with frustration.

She'd wiggled around, tossed and turned, glared at the ceiling and hadn't been able to get comfortable. The only bright spot of a night spent in his bed without Hank was the fact that his cool, beach scent still lingered in his sheets. Samantha had breathed that in, had pulled it deep into her lungs and let the very essence of his smell permeate her body. Then and only then had she felt marginally better.

Despite the fact that her drink with Jamie hadn't been an overwhelming bone-melting success, he'd asked her to go jet-skiing this afternoon and she'd accepted. Hank, she knew, would be unequivocally irritated, but he'd simply have to suck it up. She'd spent the entire day hunched over his damned computer, hadn't even been able to get out on the sand this afternoon. She'd ordered a calamari plate from the kitchen and had snuck back to their room and taken her antihistamine. To her surprise, Hank had walked in right when she'd popped it into her mouth and she'd nearly choked. When he'd quirked a questioning brow, she'd told him she had a headache. He seemed to accept that explanation, though he'd continued to stare at her suspiciously.

Of course, he probably wouldn't have thought a thing in the world about her taking that pill if she hadn't looked so damned guilty. He already suspected something was up. The last thing she needed to do was give him any more hints as to what it could be.

Samantha finished up, closed out the program and stood. As promised, Hank had taken care of getting her ingredients for the fried chicken cook off and they planned to brush up on her poultry skills this evening after the dinner rush.

A glance at her watch told her she had fifteen minutes before she had to meet Jamie in the foyer. That would give her just enough time to eat a couple handfuls of honey-roasted pine nuts—more sex diet food—and freshen up. Her muscles ached from sitting behind a desk all day and she was anxious to work the kinks out. A race across the gulf should be just the ticket.

Samantha double-timed it to their room and took a moment to pull her hair up, otherwise it would whip all over her face and blind her while they were on the water. She swiftly changed, applied sunblock and a little lipstick. Though she wasn't the least bit hungry, she grabbed a pack of nuts and ate them as she made the return trip to the lobby. She couldn't risk skipping so much as a snack while she was on this diet—couldn't risk her current elevated phero-mone level, otherwise her sex appeal would sink back down to its normal woefully nonexistent level.

Jamie had beaten her to the foyer and he greeted her with a ready smile. "You ready?" he asked.

"Ready for what?"

The answering grin which had leapt to her lips froze as Hank's frosty tone registered. Samantha turned to see him behind the front desk. She smiled, lifted her chin. "Jamie and I are going jet-skiing."

Hank glanced at Jamie and came around the desk. "Oh? You're finished straightening out the reservation system, then?" he asked innocently. Too innocently.

A prickle of annoyance surfaced. She'd agreed to help him, however since she wasn't a paid employee she didn't appreciate the implied recrimination. "No, not quite."

Hank hummed under his breath and affected a slightly bemused look she itched to wipe from his face. "I see."

"I don't believe you do," Samantha replied tightly. But you will. "It's going to take me the rest of this week to get that mess sorted out, Hank. I'm certain I explained that to you. I'm also certain that I've explained something else to you," she said meaningfully. "So I'll see you later." The last she forced through slightly gritted teeth.

Hank expelled a breath, rubbed the back of his neck. "When will you be back?"

Samantha's eyes narrowed fractionally and she cocked her head. "Whenever I get ready, *Daddy*."

Jamie chuckled. "She'll be back in plenty of time to fry chicken, if that's what you're worried about." His voice rang with lazy amusement, and something else, something that only Hank seemed privy to because his expression immediately blackened with displeasure.

Samantha's brow furrowed. How had Jamie known about she and Hank's plans for this evening? She knew she hadn't told him. She considered the men before her once more and decided her first assessment had been dead-on—apparently, they *were* friends. She made a mental note to get the skinny from Jamie this afternoon.

"I'm not the one who should be worrying," Hank replied. His voice was amiable enough, but held an unmistakable edge.

"Lighten up, Hank." He shot him a look over his shoulder that was loaded with equal parts humor and innuendo. "I promise I'll take good care of her."

Samantha grinned. Well, that certainly sounded promising. She cast one last look at Hank as she let Jamie lead her out the door, then immediately wished she hadn't. Hank looked more than furious, more than thwarted...he looked curiously vulnerable.

9:15

Hank glanced at the clock and felt a vein throb in his forehead. She should have been back fifteen minutes ago. He'd had the entire afternoon to stalk around and seethe, the entire afternoon to wonder just what the hell it was they were doing. Jamie, damn him, would *so* pay for this, Hank decided as a tortured laugh pushed into his throat.

Last night when Samantha had finally come in, Hank had gone to Jamie and explained the situation.

Again.

Forcibly.

She leaves here in the same condition she arrived in. She is not a plaything, a toy, or a potential lover. She's mine. If you touch her, I'll kill you. He couldn't have made it plainer, right? And yet, here Hank sat in his deserted kitchen with only his bad mood and a couple of whole fryers for company.

He'd known about the jet-skiing trip—Jamie had told him—yet for some reason, he'd thought that Jamie would cancel, or that Sam would be so caught up in fixing his reservation system that she would. But he should have known better. Her quest for an orgasm would take precedence over his computer woes, no matter how much Sam enjoyed a good challenge. She could be annoyingly single-minded, a trait he normally admired, but in this particular case, didn't.

Granted, he'd kept her busy with the reservation system—though he knew it was a sneaky, horrible thing for him to do, he'd gone behind her this afternoon and completely undone the progress she'd made—but he didn't think he'd be able to keep her tied to the thing indefinitely.

Luckily he wouldn't have to, because starting tonight, he planned to be her lover, to give her that orgasm she so desperately wanted. It was hard to believe that a mini-lifetime of restraint would come to this, but it was, and he was utterly powerless to stop it. Didn't want to. He was willing to risk their friendship, his heart and her rejection—though he refused to consider the idea on principal, she could simply tell him to go to hell. He didn't think that she would, because he firmly intended to give her the seduction she wanted, but it was still not out of the realm of possibility.

But he couldn't stand the alternative—the someone else. Hank swallowed. He simply couldn't let it happen.

She'd been asleep last night when he'd gotten back and simply knowing that she was in his bed, beneath his sheets had all but driven him mad with lust. He pulled in a shallow breath as the vision swam into focus once more. Naked limbs, bare breasts and all those strawberry-blond curls fanned out across a stark white pillow.

Hank had taken a moment to look at her, just look at her, and a curious emotion had swelled into his throat and forced him to swallow. One toned leg had been slung over the covers and he'd caught a flash of pink on her toes. He'd never considered a woman's feet before, but at the moment, he'd been consumed with the need to start at her vulnerable instep and lick his way up her body. Up her slim calf, over that soft skin behind her knee, then farther still until he reached the tender inside of her creamy thigh.

At this point, Hank had become less concerned about that curious swelling in this throat and more concerned with the swelling in his boxers, because once he imagined licking her thigh, a man didn't get much closer to the grand prize without imagining fastening his mouth upon what lay at the juncture of those thighs, then planting himself firmly between them.

One vision had led to another and it had been all he could do not to recreate that vision—in the flesh. With her. All he could do to simply turn away and lie down on that damned uncomfortable couch. He'd barely gotten a wink of sleep, had been in a foul mood all day as a result and now— Hank pulled in a deep breath, then blew it out with a whoosh. Now, she was late.

Because she was with Jamie, his friend she intended to seduce.

Hank muttered a long steady stream of hot oaths and, for lack of something better to hit, knocked the hell out of the chicken.

"I've heard of men choking the chicken, but that's the first time I've ever seen a guy spank one," came a droll feminine voice from the doorway.

Hank blushed, annoyed. "You're late."

Samantha strolled over, sat her purse down on the kitchen table, then lowered herself into the chair opposite him. Her hair was delightfully mussed and she brought the scent of cool, salty air and her particularly fruity fragrance with her. Her eyes twinkled with humor. "I wasn't aware that I was punching a time clock."

Hank grunted. There were a lot of things she wasn't aware of. Like the fact he wanted to pump her until her eyes rolled back in her head and the thought of taking any other lover was a distant memory. "Did you have a good time?"

Samantha slipped a sandal off and gingerly massaged the instep he'd been fantasizing about. "Yes, I did."

Hank got the feeling that she purposely didn't elaborate. He waited a beat, then said, "Well, what did you do?"

An exaggerated frown creased her brow. "You mean before or after we had sex?"

Hank vaulted to his feet. *"What?"*

To his supreme irritation, Samantha cracked up. "Sit down," she chuckled. "Sheesh. I was only joking. Lighten up, would ya? We had a good time. That was all. End of story."

Lighten up? *Lighten up?* His entire frontal lobe threatened to explode from his forehead and she had the nerve to tell him to lighten up?

Sam's laughter tittered into a sigh and she frowned thoughtfully. "Hell, so far he hasn't even kissed me, a point I plan to rectify myself the next time we go out. I wouldn't have pegged him for the hesitant type, but—" her pointed gaze slammed into his and a wry grin curled those sweetly lush lips "—I'm getting the distinct impression that he's been given a you-can-look-but-don't-touch-order from a certain mutual friend whom I've asked to butt out.'' Samantha laid her hand upon his arm. ''Look I know that this is difficult for you, but—''

Hank snorted grimly. ''You have no idea.''

''But you're going to have to let me grow up, Hank.'' Her sympathetic yet determined gaze searched his. ''I'm not really your little sister, and while the big-protective-brother act is appreciated, it's really not necessary.''

Little sister? She was still laboring under the incorrect assumption that he looked at her like a little sister? Hell, even Tina—who, quite frankly, wasn't the brightest bulb on the tree—had figured out Hank's problem. She'd blasted him with the unhappy truth this afternoon after he'd wrongly taken his frustration out on her.

Ironically, the only person who *hadn't* deduced the obvious was Samantha.

Hank's gaze slid to where her hand lay innocently upon his arm. That simple innocuous touch literally made his arm tingle, sent a white-hot bolt of heat straight to his groin.

''What do you mean, *you plan to rectify?*'' Hank asked, ignoring everything else that she'd said.

''Exactly what I said.'' She stood, snagged the chicken and moved it to the battered work island. ''Since he's obviously been told not to make a move on me, I'll just make the move myself.'' She shrugged lightly and a secret smile rolled around her lips. ''A preemptive strike, so to speak.''

A dull roaring had commenced in his head. He had to unclench his jaw in order to speak, an increasingly frequent occurrence. "If you read that in one of those magazines you brought along with your arsenal of rubbers, then you're making a grave mistake." Hank leaned back in his chair and made a valiant effort to look rational. No small feat when every cell in his body had atrophied with dread. "Men don't like pushy women."

Samantha neatly butchered the chicken. "Would you get me that buttermilk mixture out of the fridge? And, I won't be pushy—I'll be seductive. There's a difference—" her lips quirked with dry humor "—but then you've never been able to appreciate subtlety."

Hank did as she asked, set the bowl on the island and watched her efficiently slide the chicken into the mixture. Though he knew what had to be done, finding the right words to frame the conversation was proving damned difficult. She was right—subtlety wasn't his strong suit and, quite honestly, even if it had been, he didn't think he'd be able to find a subtle way of telling her what he had to say. With any other woman, simply moving into seduction mode would have worked, but he couldn't do that with Sam—she wasn't any other woman.

"That'll need to soak for half an hour," she said, oblivious to his secret torture. "I'll go ahead and mix up the flour and spices." She pulled a cast-iron skillet from the rack above the work island and set it on the stove, then rummaged around in the cabinets until she found the oil.

Hank's throat went inexplicably dry. This was a whole lot harder than the ever thought it would be. He rubbed the back of his neck. "You know, Sam, I've been thinking," he said, striving for a light tone that by no means matched the lead in his belly.

She hummed a response, presumably still foraging for ingredients.

With effort, Hank swallowed. "J-just how bad do you want that orgasm?"

She snorted darkly. "Bad."

Hank forced a long-suffering sigh. "Okay, then."

Samantha chuckled again and shot him a side-long glance. Those bright green eyes twinkled. "I don't recall asking for your permission."

A laugh stuttered out of his throat. He pushed an uncomfortable smile into place and said the one thing guaranteed to change their relationship forever—and it damn sure wasn't subtle. "I'm not giving it—I'm offering my services."

8

SAMANTHA MOMENTARILY STILLED, certain that she hadn't heard him correctly. *"What?"*

Hank shifted uneasily, shrugged. "I said, I'm offering my services."

If he'd told her he was a gay, cross-dressing hermaphrodite who was into S&M, she couldn't have been any more astounded. Samantha blinked, attempted to absorb what he'd just said—which was difficult given the roaring in her head—and the implications of that shocking statement. A rush of conflicting emotions ranging from elation to outrage rushed through her, each of them scrambling for purchase in her suddenly whirling brain.

Luckily self-preservation won out and humor bullied its way forward to save her. He couldn't be serious. He was simply trying to thwart her again…right? *Right,* she mentally confirmed, not daring to imagine that he wasn't. It was too painful, too close to what she'd always wanted, and oh sweet Lord, so very, very tempting.

Samantha chuckled under her breath and shot him a sardonic look. "Your services?"

Hank swallowed again. "Right."

"What sort of services?" she asked just to torture him. Honestly, she knew he'd had an unreasonable aversion to her taking a lover, but *this?* This gave a whole new meaning to the old take-one-for-the-team phrase.

He cleared his throat. "Whatever kind you deem necessary."

Various scenarios of what she would deem necessary obligingly tripped through her mind and in every instance she and Hank were naked. The tops of her thighs tingled and every ounce of moisture evaporated from her mouth. She pulled a bowl from the cabinet and set it on the work island, then dumped a generous amount of flour into the container.

She drew in a shuddering breath, summoned a composure she didn't feel. "Well, thanks, Hank," she said for lack of anything better. "That's truly a unique offer...but I'm afraid I'll have to pass."

Hank had leaned against the island, but at her remark he pushed off, seemingly agitated and bewildered. "You'll pass? Why? Why would you pass? You said you wanted an orgasm and I've offered to give you one. Hell, I'll give you a dozen. Why in God's name would you pass?"

"Because you're being an idiot," she said flatly. Why was he doing this? Did he have any idea how painful this was for her?

His eyes widened. "An idiot?"

"Yes," she said, exasperated. She shook salt, pepper and a little paprika into the mix and began to stir it up. Flour poofed out of the bowl, evidence of her agitation. "An idiot. The whole point of me finding a lover for myself is just that—finding someone for myself who *wants* to be with me. I'm touched that you're willing to…sacrifice yourself like this, but I assure you, it's not necessary." She snorted, unwilling to look at him. She set the spoon aside and crossed her arms over her chest. "I'm not interested in being your pity-project, Hank." Or, more accurately, a pity-fuck.

"Who said anything about a pity-project? It's simple and you're making it complicated. You want an orgasm, then I'll give you one," Hank insisted heatedly, jabbing himself in the chest for emphasis. "Me, dammit. No one else."

Good grief, if she didn't know better she'd swear he sounded downright possessive. Jealous even. Though she knew it was pure folly on her part, she couldn't help but be a little flattered, couldn't help but wish it were true.

"Well, that's really not up to you, now is it?"

"Sam—"

She exhaled mightily. "Hank, listen. This is really not necessary. It's not. You're taking all of this entirely too seriously. If I'd known you were going to be so damned overwrought, I wouldn't have told you my plans. Listen to yourself," she told him. "Are you even hearing what you're saying?"

"Yes, dammit, I am," he returned hotly. "Are you?"

Samantha chuckled under her breath. "I'm hearing it, but I'm not believing it."

Hank shoved a hand through his hair. "Why the hell not?"

She couldn't believe they were having this conversation. Frustration peaked. "Haven't you listened to anything I've told you?" Samantha all but wailed. "I want to be with someone who *wants* me. If I just wanted an orgasm without desire, I could masturbate—like you so helpfully pointed out—or hire a lover. In fact, I even considered it. But that's—"

His expression blackened with outrage. "Hire a lover—"

"—not what I want," she continued doggedly. "I want to be *wanted*, Hank," Samantha told him and resisted the urge to howl. "And we both know that you don't want me—you just don't want me to be with anyone else."

Hank came around the island and stood next to her. She could feel the heat rolling off him in waves, could feel his frustration pinging her like sonar. "You're only half right," he said softly, his voice a deep decadent rumble.

Samantha stilled and the storm that had been

steadily brewing inside her quieted. Her heart rate geared into overdrive. "What are you talking about? What part did I get wrong?"

Hank grasped her shoulders and turned her around to face him. "The part where you said that I don't want you."

Her foolish heart leapt—a heart usually did before it broke. She swallowed tightly. "Don't lie. You don't have to do this."

An anguished laugh burst from his throat and those sea-blue eyes gleamed with abject desperation. "Sam, I'm not lying. I've wanted you for…forever. For years."

For years? Sam thought, utterly stunned. But she didn't dare let herself believe him. That road led to madness and heartache—hers. She shook her head. "This is ridiculous," she said faintly, barely able to summon the strength to speak. "Why are you doing this? Why are you telling me all this? Why now? If you wanted me before, why didn't you ever say anything?"

Hank sobered. "Because I didn't want to jeopardize our friendship."

"But you do now?" She didn't have any trouble believing the reason—she'd kept her feelings to herself for the very same argument. But she still didn't get it. What made *now* different? If it were true—and God how she wished it were—then what had happened to make him admit his feelings now?

A frown wriggled between her brows. It just didn't make any sense. Was too much to take in.

"No, I don't—your friendship means everything to me, Sam. It always has. But I can't let you do this. Not here. Not now. Not with anybody else. I know it's crazy, but I— I can't turn it off. I haven't been able to turn it off since the summer you turned eighteen." A broken laugh stuttered out of his mouth. "Hell, I almost kissed you. Don't you remember?"

Sam nodded, swallowed. Of course she remembered. She'd never been able to forget. "But you didn't. You stopped."

"Well, it wasn't because I wanted to, believe me. I wanted to kiss you more than anything." His gaze dropped to her mouth and traced her lips, making a quivery sensation flutter through her belly. "Still do. That fruity scent of yours drives me nuts," he all but growled. "I look at you and all I can think about is…giving you that orgasm you want." His nostrils flared as he dragged in a harsh breath. "I can't stand the thought of any other guy touching you. It makes my skin itch, makes me want to put my fist through a wall." He paused. "You want to know why, but there's really no why to this, Sam. Believe me," he laughed darkly, shook his head. "I've tried to figure it out. It just *is*."

He was wrong, Samantha thought as her well-thought-out plan got sucked into the confusing chaos of this moment.

There was a why, he just didn't know it—the sex diet.

A finger of dread prodded her belly and what little air had made it into her lungs stuttered out in a soundless gasp of alarm. He might have wanted her before, but he'd always been able to keep it in check. Had never acted on the attraction.

Until now.

Until she'd practically turned herself into a walking pheromone.

Samantha couldn't decide whether to be disappointed or thrilled, couldn't make her brain assemble anything close to a coherent thought, much less a solution. She didn't know what to do, what to say. She was utterly flabbergasted, completely at a loss. The fact that he'd wanted her for almost as long as she'd wanted him should have been a coup, a moment of glory, and yet it wasn't because she'd essentially tricked him into confessing his feelings. If she hadn't gone on this sex diet, would he have ever told her the truth? He'd managed to keep it to himself for years in order to safeguard their friendship, but he was throwing caution to the wind now? Was willing to jeopardize that friendship now?

"Well?" Hank asked impatiently.

Samantha blinked, yanked from her fractured thoughts, and looked up. "Well what?"

A faint, vulnerable smile tugged at the corner of his mouth. "What do you think? I've bared my soul here, Sam. You can't just leave me hanging."

"I, uh... I don't know, Hank." She sighed, shoved a shaky hand through her hair. "There's a lot to consider."

His smile faded somewhat. "Like whether or not you're attracted to me?"

An ironic chuckle fizzed up her throat before she could check it. Jeez, she was obviously a much better actress than she'd ever given herself credit for if he thought that was the reason she didn't jump on his offer. Jump him, for that matter.

The minute his confession had registered, every cell in her body had gone warm and a sluggish heat had begun to wind through her limbs. A steady pulse beat at the apex of her thighs and she'd had to make a concerted effort to keep her gaze away from his unbelievably carnal mouth. Her nipples had hardened and presently strained against the flimsy fabric of her bra. She'd like nothing better than to shed said bra, swiftly remove his shirt and rub her aching nipples across his powerfully muscled chest.

"No," Samantha said, neatly avoiding that land mine question. "I was thinking about our friendship."

Hank rocked back lightly on his heels and a

smidge of his former confidence clung to his renewed smile. "So you *are* attracted to me, then?"

Sam felt her lips twitch. He had the tenacity of a bulldog with a soup bone and seemed determined to pry the truth out of her. "You're missing the point. What you're suggesting would permanently alter our relationship."

He sobered, blew out a breath. "Samantha, I permanently altered our relationship when I told you how I felt. It'll always be there between us now. I'm sorry if I've made you uncomfortable...but I just couldn't let you do this." He emitted a low frustrated growl and his gaze caressed her lips. "It's making me crazy."

He was right, she knew. Yet still she hesitated. She chewed her bottom lip. "Be that as it may, it's still a lot to consider, Hank."

"Fine," Hank told her. "But consider this while you're at it."

Before she could form any sort of reply, Hank stepped forward, gently framed her face with his tanned hands, and swiftly lowered his mouth to hers.

An electric shock of pleasure hummed up her spine and her lips parted in a delighted *oh* of surprise, which Hank immediately used to his advantage. He simultaneously slid his tongue into her mouth and shifted closer to her, burying his fingers in her hair and angling her head so that he could slant his lips more firmly over hers.

Swept up in a tornado of instant sensation, Samantha's knees buckled and she melted against him. A flash of heat shot up her legs and pooled in her sex.

His kiss was everything she'd ever dreamed it would be and more.

Hot and thrilling, dark and seductive. He fed and suckled, teased, nipped and plundered. He tasted like beer and sin, of forbidden pleasures and dreams come true. His woefully familiar frame pressed against hers, fusing her to him from ankle to mouth and it felt so right, so heart-wrenchingly perfect. She'd waited a lifetime for this moment and it had been unquestionably worth the wait.

Samantha kissed him back, put every ounce of repressed longing into the melding of their mouths, every iota of feeling she possessed. She chased his tongue with hers, played a heady game of seek and retreat. His scent, an intriguing combination of beach and man, rushed into her nostrils, drugged her, made every part of her body sing with need.

She slid her hands up and over his chest, felt him tremble beneath her palms, then slid them farther still, up over his heavily muscled shoulders and into the silky hair at his nape. She ate his sigh, savored it on her tongue, felt a hard bulge prod against her belly and the realization sent an intoxicating feminine rush of power flooding through her because she knew what it meant.

He wanted her—*truly wanted her.*

The knowledge burrowed into her heart, made her eyes water with sweet emotion.

Before she could get too caught up in the sentiment, Hank deepened the kiss, slowed it down, yet made it all the more intensifying, lush and provocative. He made a low, growling sound, a masculine purr of pleasure that vibrated something deep inside of her, made her press herself more tightly against him, made her squirm in her skin, made a hot, itchy heat concentrate in her womb and pulse in her moist sex. Her palms tingled and every inch of her body softened as languid ribbons of tangled need and heat wove through her.

That orgasm she so desperately needed hovered just barely out of reach. She suppressed a whimper and absently rubbed the back of her itching wrist across Hank's collar.

Hank murmured a nonsensical sound against her lips, part groan, part growl and sucked her bottom lip. He anchored one hand around her waist, drawing her even closer, then slid his hand up her side, over her quivering ribs and ultimately settled it gently over her breast. "I can make you come right now," he told her. "Just say yes."

Oh, God, how she wanted to. A sigh stuttered out of her mouth and into his as the exquisite sensation eddied through her. She pushed her achy nipple farther into his palm and whimpered when he thumbed it through her shirt.

"I'll give you every kind of orgasm you can imagine, as many as you want, I promise." He licked her neck, creating a blaze of sensation. "Starting right now. Say yes."

Samantha whimpered, strained toward him, lifted her foot and used her toe to nudge an itch above her opposite ankle. A fleeting grimace of irritation in the midst of the most pleasurable sensation in her life. He was offering her everything she'd ever wanted—him. And he was right. The moment he'd told her how he felt, their relationship changed. She wanted— She needed—

Hank found her mouth once more, kissed her deeply. His hand left her breast and slowly trekked toward her weeping sex. He slipped his hand beneath her waistband, then beneath her panties, and the first brush of those talented fingers against her drenched curls made a startled cry break from her lips.

His hot breath fanned against her ear. "Say yes," he whispered. A shiver shook her. *Ahhh,* her first ever *ear*gasm, Sam thought dimly. But the thought was no more born than abandoned, when Hank shifted a smidge and his fingers found her pulsing clit. She inhaled sharply.

"Yes!" Sam cried as the real thing instantly

flooded through her. She arched her neck, felt her eyes honest-to-God roll back her in head—proof that it wasn't just an expression—as wave after wave of the most exquisite sensation she'd ever felt whipped through her. She sank her teeth into her lip, her knees all but buckled, and if Hank hadn't been leaning against her, she would have undoubtedly slid to the floor in a boneless satisfied heap at his feet.

Hank continued to softly stroke her, milking the sensation for all it was worth. A satisfied chuckle sounded against her ear. "If that's all it takes, baby, then I'm one lucky guy."

An unpleasant tingling surfaced behind her ear. She frowned absently, dragged reluctantly from her postorgasm euphoria and scratched until the irritation subsided.

Hank nipped at her earlobe. "Samantha...you're scratching again."

"Mmm?"

"You're scratching again," he repeated, his voice a deep, sexy rasp.

A flag of warning waved in her thoughts, but her mind was too foggy to discern much less heed the alarm. She turned her head and found Hank's mouth again, fed from it until her senses whirled and his lips weren't enough. She kissed his jaw, the vulnerable side of his neck and then tugged at his earlobe, subjecting him to the same sort of provocative tongue-treatment he'd just given her. His breath came out in a harsh, startled gasp, then a soft wicked chuckle rumbled lightly from his smiling lips.

Samantha felt her own lips curl as she snuggled even closer to him, licked a path up down the side of neck and back up over his jaw. Hank had kindled a fire in her loins and every part of her ached for more. She wanted another orgasm and right now seemed like just as good a time as any. The back of her leg tingled with a determined itch, dragging her momentarily from the swaddling sugar-spun haze of desire. She grimaced, angrily lifted her leg to scratch her calf—and accidentally kneed Hank in the groin.

Hank's startled eyes all but crossed, a guttural groan tore from his throat, the color leached from his face and, hands clutched protectively over his crotch, he crumpled to the floor.

Horrified, Samantha gasped, scratched her leg and dropped to her knees beside him. "Oh, God, Hank," she moaned miserably. "Omigod, omigod, omigod. I'm so sorry!" She wanted to touch him, help him—anything— but was utterly helpless, at a complete loss. Who knew what kind of first aid one needed to administer in such a situation?

Hank's face was contorted in pain and he curled into the fetal position. "No...problem," he squeaked brokenly. Veins stuck out on his neck. "I'll…be all right…in a…minute."

Samantha fidgeted miserably, worriedly chewed her bottom lip. "I'm so sorry."

"Quite…all right," he assured breathlessly. "What's…with the…damned scratching?"

Scratching? Samantha wondered. Oh, hell. Her antihistamine. She'd forgotten to take it after dinner, and she'd eaten enough shrimp to bankrupt Bubba Gump. She'd meant to take it when she got back, but they'd been running late and Hank had beaten her to the kitchen. Then he'd started that whole I-want-you bit and kissed her and she'd had her first ever orgasm…

And it had been the last thing on her mind.

Hell, who was she kidding? Samantha inwardly snorted. It hadn't been anywhere near her mind, *she'd* been completely out of her mind. Hank's tongue had been in her ear and his big warm hand had been playing at her breast, then in her panties and every coherent thought—every intellectual tendency—had fled from her brain.

Jeez, how could she have been so stupid? How could she have let this happen? She'd finally managed to dredge up a little sex appeal—had finally— miraculously—gotten Hank Masterson to confess his latent desire—and she was going to blow it by being an absentminded moron. She needed professional help. She really did.

Samantha blew out a small breath. "Mosquito bites," she lied. Her gaze searched his pain-racked face and she winced. "Oh, Hank, I'm so sorry. So very, very sorry. Can I get you an ice pack—"

His eyes widened in horror.

"—or anything?" she finished quickly. "Anything else?"

He cut her a crafty look and a wicked gleam danced in his still-hurting gaze. "There is... something," he said consideringly.

Samantha leaned forward. "What? Anything."

He managed a faint grin. "You could kiss it and make it better," he murmured silkily.

Samantha felt a flush of heat start at her ankles, race to her hairline and tried to tell herself it was embarrassment. She might have pulled it off, too, if she hadn't been struck momentarily dumb by the image of doing just that to him. Pulling every inch of him into her mouth and tasting him until he roared with satisfaction.

Somehow she conjured a droll smile. "Anything else?"

Hank's hopeful smile faded, but his eyes twinkled all the same. He groaned and shifted gingerly into a sitting position. "How 'bout helping me up?"

With her help, he lurched to his feet and leaned against the island. His tight lips were white with pain and beads of sweat dotted his forehead.

"I'm so sorry," she repeated again.

"I'll, uh, be fine." Hank shifted, winced, but a faint satisfied smile clung to his lips. "So…are you through considering?"

She'd say, Sam thought. It would sort of be like shutting the barn door after the cow had gotten out at this point. Still, a part of her wanted to hesitate. In less than ten minutes, thanks in part to this sex diet, she'd been given the opportunity to have her heart's desire—Hank Masterson. But should she do it? Any more than she already had? Granted he'd been right when he said their relationship had just changed. There had been no doubt about that, and there was no doubt that the orgasm he'd just treated her to would forever change the dynamic of their relationship.

But there was a vast difference between a little finger action—albeit climactic action—and sex. She was in for the penny…but didn't know if she was ready to ante up the pound. There was a great deal at stake—namely her heart. And when she went off this sex diet, undoubtedly Hank's mind would clear, he'd wonder what the hell had happened, why he'd acted on this attraction now when he never had before, and they'd never be right again. They'd become strangers overnight, awkward and miserable. Years invested in a friendship that would be too flawed to survive. Did she want that? Could she live with it? Better still, could she refuse what he'd offered?

She knew the answer to that as well as she knew her own name. Samantha heaved an internal sigh and her gaze slid to where Hank stood. Need and affection broadsided her, and a lump inexplicably formed in her throat even as her womb filled with an achy, needy, desperate heat.

No, she couldn't refuse. Wouldn't despite the possibly disastrous consequences. She'd wanted Hank longer than forever, more than her next breath, and tonight he'd given her everything she'd ever wanted.

To be wanted—by him.

To be kissed—by him.

An orgasm—by him.

And not only that, but he'd promised her more. Every kind of orgasm she could imagine, as many as she wanted. Should she put a stop to this madness? Most definitely. Would she? Most definitely not.

She finally nodded. "I'm through considering."

"And?"

She steepled her fingers beneath her chin. "Are you sure you want to go through with this?"

Hank exhaled slowly. "Sure that it's not a mistake? No. Sure that I want you anyway? Yes."

He'd summed that up neatly, Sam thought, because that was precisely how she felt as well. At least they were on the same page. Though trepidation shook her tummy, she nevertheless felt a hesitant smile quiver on her lips. Her gaze tangled with his. "Then I say...yes."

Hank chuckled, drew her to him. "If I remember correctly, you already did."

Sam blushed. Indeed she had. And she looked forward to saying it again and again.

9

Despite the fact that hours had passed and indecision and doubt over his actions still plagued him, despite the knowledge that he'd permanently altered possibly the most important friendship in his life, and despite the fact that his nuts had been shoved a good foot up into his abdomen, Hank didn't regret kissing Sam, making her come, didn't regret finally telling her the truth about how he felt.

He couldn't, not when nothing had ever felt more right.

In fact, though he'd never been prone to sentiment, had never been what one could call the romantic type, Hank had been curiously affected— some unnamed emotion had swelled into his chest even as a bolt of white-hot heat had shot to his loins—and he'd been hit with the almost overwhelming realization that *this* was what he'd been waiting for, *this* had been what he'd unwittingly needed.

The moment he'd pressed his lips to hers he'd felt it. Her sweet breath had sighed into his mouth, then she'd sagged against him and from that point on, his cognitive thinking had evaporated and pure animal instinct had taken over. Had she not kneed him in the groin—what in God's was with that infernal scratching? Hank wondered irritably—he would have undoubtedly set her on top of the kitchen island, spread her delectable thighs and plunged in and out of her until they both screamed with the force of release. He wondered if she realized that's what he would have done if she hadn't incapacitated him, if she had any idea that what he felt for her went well beyond typical lust, need and desire.

It wasn't a question of him wanting her now—he had to have her.

And she had to win this damned contest. Rather than continuing what they'd started, they'd fried chicken. Hank grinned. Not what he'd wanted to do, but it hadn't been unpleasant, either, because he'd been with Sam. Nothing was ever unpleasant with Sam.

Though he wasn't ready to dig around his brain in search of an explanation as to why he was so desperate for her to move back—an emotional revelation he wasn't quite ready to deal with would undoubtedly surface should he do too much excavation—Hank desperately wanted her to move back here. He'd been unexpectedly delighted when she mentioned moving back, but that delight had morphed into outright necessity within a matter of seconds, then into full-blown need within a minute.

He wanted her here. With him.

Right now he had to focus on making that happen and he'd sort the why of it out later. Action now, think later. Sounded like a plan. Probably not the best one, but it was all he could come up with at the moment. A short ironic laugh burst from his throat. Hell, given what he'd been through with her over the past twenty-four hours, it was nothing short of a miracle that he could string two thoughts together.

In addition to being emotionally fried, the majority of his blood had been pooled south of his waistband. His brain was dehydrated. Hank speared his hand through his hair, rubbed his eyes with the flat of his palms until he saw little black stars dance behind his lids.

"Correct me if I'm wrong, but isn't there a gorgeous woman in your bed?"

Hank looked up and blinked, gratefully accepted the longneck Jamie handed in his direction. "Yeah, she's there."

"And yet you're here." With a sigh, Jamie settled himself into the chair next to Hank. "You want her, so what gives? Let me guess. Noble second thoughts."

Hank shook his head. There was nothing noble

about his thoughts. "Not second thoughts, just thoughts," Hank clarified.

"What's there to think about?"

Hank tipped his bottle up and all but drained it. "Like whether or not it's a good idea to sleep with your best friend."

Jamie's chuckle sounded in the darkness. "I'm flattered, Hank, but let me make it easy for you— I'm not interested."

"I wasn't talking about you." He snorted. "Arrogant bastard," he muttered, unable to quell a laugh.

Jamie laughed. "Personally, I think that you've been thinking about this entirely too long. You've thought it to death. Do it already." He grunted under his breath. "Hell, she's obviously crazy about you."

It was utterly pathetic how his heart jumped. Hank stilled, affected a you're-full-of-shit expression. "What makes you say that?"

Jamie shrugged. "It's simple, really, and if you'd been paying closer attention you would have noticed. You're all she talks about."

"Maybe to you, but I'm all the two of you have in common," he argued. "It's only natural that she'd talk about me to you."

"No," Jamie hedged, giving his head a hesitant shake. "It's more than that. If I had to guess, I'd say she's been carrying a torch for quite some time.''

Hank mulled that over and tried to make the theory fit. Could Jamie be right? Could Samantha have secretly had a thing for him all these years and him never know it? Up until this week, he would have scoffed at the idea, would have insisted that he knew Samantha better than anyone and, had there ever been any sort of romantic feelings on her part, he would have noticed.

Now, however, he wasn't so sure. He rolled the idea around his brain. Hank supposed Jamie could be right. There certainly hadn't been any doubt about her wanting him. Between that kiss and the subsequent instant screaming orgasm, he knew she wanted him. Come to think of it, she'd never denied wanting him. And there had been something so sweet, so reverent in the way that she'd initially clung to him. The moment had lasted but a second, but he'd noticed it all the same. Then she'd been on fire, had kissed him with more needy enthusiasm than he'd ever experienced.

Of course, that could have simply been the result of her admittedly neglected hormones. Who was to say that if Jamie had kissed her, she wouldn't have reacted in the exact same way? The thought didn't sit well, so rather than ponder it, Hank beat the notion out of his head. He couldn't think about her kissing Jamie or being with Jamie in any capacity—

with any man—which was what had prompted him into telling her how he felt in the first place, what had prompted him to overthrow years of cautious behavior and promise her countless orgasms.

The iced tea and fried chicken bake-off was tomorrow at noon, then the actual *Belle* pageant would be hosted in the evening. Hank fully intended for her to win—was almost desperate enough to pull a few strings to ensure that very end. Sneaky and underhanded, yes. But if it brought her back to him, then the end would justify the means, right? As it happened, he knew both of the secret judges. He filed the idea away for future consideration because another more tantalizing thought had pushed into his mind—the ultimate celebration.

He'd asked Samantha to dinner tomorrow night, and had planned something really special for her. If there were any lingering doubts as to his sincerity—as to how much he wanted her—they would be swiftly dispelled tomorrow evening after that pageant because he fully intended to give her a night she would never forget.

"THIS IS STUPID," Samantha hissed, batting Hank away from her as he tried to wrestle her into a frilly apron. "I'm not wearing it."

"It's not stupid, it's genius." He pulled the garment over her head, whirled her around and tied the sash. "It'll make you stand out."

"It'll make me look like an idiot. I'm not supposed to wear this." The *Belle* contestants had met with the pageant director this morning. They'd been encouraged to dress casually, like they would at home for this particular part of the contest. Samantha glanced down at the apron Hank had found for her and stifled the burgeoning need to scream. She'd *never* wear this.

Before she could argue with Hank any further about the ridiculous cherry-printed apron, Samantha was distracted by a curious weight around her neck and the tantalizing brush of Hank's fingers over her nape. She repressed a shiver, then reached for her throat and gasped. *Pearls?* "What the hell are you doing?"

"Trying to help you, dammit," Hank snapped. "Now hold still. You've only got a few minutes before you have to present your plate and drink to the judges."

"They're not going to like the taste of my chicken any better if I look like a June Cleaver reject," Samantha said through gritted teeth.

"Wrong. Packaging is everything—including how we package you. You want to win, right? There," Hank said, finally securing the clasp. He shoved a pair of red pumps at her. "Now put these on."

Samantha shook her head. Oh, no. Not no, but hell, no. "Hank, I—"

"Put them on."

She glared at him, heaved a long-suffering sigh and did as he told her. Honestly, she didn't know what had come over him. Last night when they'd finished up in the kitchen, he'd seemed pretty calm compared to what he'd been since she'd gotten into town. Even after The Orgasm—her toes involuntarily curled at the reminder—and the subsequent groin accident, while there had been a wee bit of tension between them, it hadn't been as a result of what had happened between them, but rather what *hadn't* happened. Not an awkward sort of tension, but sexual tension.

Ironically she'd missed an itch she'd been desperately waiting to scratch over an itch that could have been prevented if she'd only taken her damned antihistamine. The idea made her want to throw her head back and wail. Stomp her feet and moan and cry.

Samantha knew it had probably been for the best—she'd needed to think about what Hank had said, what he'd offered and the conclusion she'd drawn as a result of that conversation. Now, hours later, though the taste of him still lingered on her lips and the pleasant hum of release still lingered in her sex, she was still not sure that she'd made the right decision.

But it felt right and she had every intention of seeing it through.

Hank was right—things would never be the same now that he'd told her how he presently felt. Granted last night, they'd moved right along without much of a problem, but as time wore on what would happen? If things didn't work out, would they be able to get past it? Had any couple in the history of the world successfully segued from friends-to-lovers-to-friends again?

Hank had essentially offered her exactly what she'd always wanted, with only one small exception—she'd get him…but only temporarily, she feared. The minute she went off the sex diet, it would all be over. It would be finished. She didn't have a single doubt about that. Her appeal would take a dramatic nosedive and he'd wonder what had happened. What had prompted his rash behavior. Then, he'd undoubtedly regret this week, and then where would they be? Sam blew out a breath as a whole new batch of uncertainties bombarded her.

Right now Hank was at the mercy of her elevated pheromones—he didn't know why he'd suddenly become attracted to her, but she did—and once the sex diet wore off and his attraction wore off right along with it, then there they'd be. Their friendship over, their lives forever changed. Either way, things would never be the same. She was damned if she did, and damned if she didn't—which was all the more reason why she'd decided that she couldn't pass up this opportunity.

Hank was her dream come true, and though it might be selfish, she didn't care that it had taken a sex diet to make him act on his attraction—she was still blown away by that little verbal bomb—but she just couldn't help herself. For the time being, she was going to pretend that everything would be fine. She wasn't going to think about what-if's, or if-only's or beyond the rest of this week. She was simply going to be what she'd always wanted to be—his.

Hank had asked her to dinner tonight and, given the way his gaze had lingered on her lips as he'd issued the invitation, she knew that he fully expected to do more than feed her. A quiet shiver moved through her, pushing a smile to her lips.

She couldn't wait.

Samantha couldn't wait to say *yes* again—and again and again and again—couldn't wait to explore that beautifully built body of his, learn each line and ridge, each freckle and mole, and have him do the same for her in turn. She wanted that bulge she'd felt eagerly nudging her belly last night lodged deep down inside her, wanted his mouth on her breast and his hands in her hair.

She wanted to taste every inch of him and use every one of those damned extra-large condoms she'd brought along. Remembered heat swirled through her belly. They'd most definitely fit him. She wanted him to make love to her sweet and slow, then hard and fast and every way in between. She wanted to experience every single carnal act her mind had ever entertained. She wanted to pack a lifetime of lovemaking into what was left of this week.

She'd always wanted him, had been in love with him for as long as she could remember. She couldn't remember her life without Hank in it and, though she knew she might possibly have to face the rest of life without him, that was a price she'd decided she'd willingly pay. Was it too high? Maybe. Probably. But the opportunity to cash in on a lifelong dream was simply more than she could pass up.

For this one, brief moment in time, Hank Masterson wanted her and she fully intended to have him.

Tonight.

The thought drew a hum of anticipation from ankle to crown, forcing her to stifle a shiver.

Hank stepped back and looked her over and she had the pleasure of watching those sea-blue eyes darken with latent desire. "You look fantastic."

Though she felt ridiculous in the apron, pearls and heels, she nevertheless felt the warmth of the compliment. "Thanks." She blew out a shaky breath. "Let's hope my chicken passes muster."

"Your chicken rocks." He frowned. "Didn't you try any?"

"Er…yeah. Of course," Samantha lied, mentally wincing at the fib. No, she hadn't. Regrettably, fried chicken wasn't a part of her sex diet. She couldn't sample it, otherwise it might wreak havoc with her pheromones and she didn't dare risk that, not when she'd miraculously managed to snag Hank's interest with them.

She'd eaten a small breakfast this morning, then, just for added insurance, she'd popped another antihistamine and had a shrimp cocktail snack. She'd try to squeeze in another chocolate candy bar before lunch, or maybe a handful of honey-roasted pine nuts, then a fish sandwich would be on the menu. Samantha grimaced. She'd grown increasingly sick of the limited fare on this damned diet and there was no way in hell—even if she wasn't allergic— that she'd be able to keep it up. She wanted a nice juicy steak, with a loaded baked potato on the side. In the mean time, she'd settle for seafood for dinner and Hank for dessert.

"Come on," Hank said, lacing his fingers through hers and tugging her out of the bedroom. "They're about to start. Tina's been on double duty, guarding your entry and scoping out the competition."

Samantha felt a wry smile tug at her lips. "Is that really necessary, Hank? This isn't the Miss America Pageant."

"Of course, it's necessary," Hank insisted.

"Sabotage, honey. Women are vicious. It happens all the time."

And he'd know, of course, Samantha thought drolly, but bit her tongue. Hank fished the walkie-talkie out of his back pocket, inadvertently giving her a sneak peek at his wonderful ass, and paged Tina. "We're on our way. How does it look?"

Static then, "There are a couple of contenders, but I don't think we have anything to worry about." She groaned miserably into the receiver. "Ugh. I'm never eating fried chicken again."

"Ten-four." Hank opened the front door and they swiftly descended the steps.

Samantha's eyes widened. "You've been making her sample all that chicken?"

"Not making her," Hank corrected amiably. "I simply suggested that she should."

She'd just bet he did, Samantha thought. Hank didn't know how to suggest anything—he ordered. Jeez, he certainly seemed to be making a big deal out of this contest. She cast him a sidelong glance and absently worried her bottom lip. She hoped he wasn't too disappointed when she lost. She'd entered, knew that she had a miniscule shot, but she had absolutely no illusions whatsoever about winning.

There were roughly fifty other candidates, all of them gorgeous—she'd covertly scoped them out this morning over breakfast and had been sick at her stomach by the time she'd had the opportunity to catalogue their tanned, toned perfection. In fact, if Hank hadn't been so gung ho about the contest this morning, she would have politely withdrawn and spared herself the humiliation. Samantha expelled a soft sigh. But he had, so that had ruled that option out.

The sand was packed with eager spectators, contestants and judges, the beach littered with towels, quilts, sand chairs and bright multicolored umbrellas. Red and white checked tables were lined across the beach, all of them laden with a sampling of chicken and iced tea from each contestant. A buzz of excitement moved through the crowd as the time drew near to judge this particular aspect of the contest.

Feeling a bit nervous, Samantha affixed her contestant number to the damned apron and found her slot occupied by Tina.

"Nice apron," Tina said with a poor-you smile. "Let me guess. Hank's idea, right?"

"Lay off the apron," Hank told her. "It's going to be what tips the odds in her favor. She's sexy, but domestic—every guy's secret fantasy. Why do you think that French Maid costume is so popular?"

Tina gave him a blank look. "Because men have no taste?"

"No," he said with exaggerated patience, "because it gives the illusion of a servant—of a woman who is there to do whatever a guy wants—and men love to be served.''

Samantha filed that little tidbit away for future reference.

''Whatever,'' Tina said. ''I'm going to find an empty piece of sand.''

''Do it behind the judges. I want you to walkie me with any developments.'' Hank, the perfection-ist, adjusted the trendy tent over her dish. ''Now relax,'' he told her, ''and remember to smile.''

She nodded, pulled in a shallow breath and re-sisted the urge to salute him. ''Right.''

Hank leaned over and brushed her cheek with a light but lingering kiss. His lips moved to her ear. ''The next time you come, I want to taste it,'' he murmured softly.

Sam gasped, startled, as a shaft of heat lodged in her womb. A mental image of Sam's blond head positioned boldly between her legs flashed behind her eyes, burned into her retinas. She blinked drunkenly. ''Think about that,'' he told her. ''Be-cause that's what I'm going to do the minute this contest is over. Forget the dress…but keep the apron.''

With that suggestive comment and everything that it implied still ringing in her ears and glaring vividly in her overwrought imagination, Hank turned and walked off. *Think about that.* As if she'd be able to think about anything else now, Sam thought, still essentially struck dumb. As soon as this contest was over, huh? Well, that gave her something to look forward to at least.

With effort, Sam directed her attention to the contest. Judges had commenced with the sampling. There were ten judges—Samantha had counted them—and each judge took five contestants.

Each judge would then pick a winner out of their allotted contestants, then narrow the contestants down to ten. When Samantha's judge, a squat chunky man who was built like a fireplug, got to her batch, she smiled a wholesome June Cleaver sort of smile and drew her shoulders back so that her breasts were shown at their most flattering angle. Her judge smiled back, took up the glass of tea, selected a chicken leg and took a generous bite.

While Samantha was trying to decide whether or not she should bat her lashes, or do any of that other coy crap she'd seen some of the other contestants try, she heard an ominous part-wheeze, part-rattling sound several contestants down and to her left. Her gaze shifted and, in the split second it took for her eyes to tell her brain what she was seeing, she'd vaulted over the table, raced down the beach—which was damned difficult in the heels Hank had insisted she put on—grabbed a choking judge around the middle and performed the Heimlich maneuver.

A series of startled gasps moved through the crowd, ending with one huge collective inhalation as a hunk of chicken the size of a golf ball exploded from the judge's mouth, arced through the air and landed with a plop in a pitcher of iced tea.

The man bent double at the waist and dragged in a long, much needed gulp of air. Other judges, contestants, and spectators hurried forward, Hank among them.

"Walter, are you going to be all right? You want me to call the paramedics?" Hank asked, his voice shaky. Concern lined his brow and he clapped a hand on the older gentleman's shoulder.

Walter shook his head. "Jesus," he wheezed, eyes streaming. "I thought for sure I was a goner." His watery gaze found Samantha's. "Thank you, young lady. I'm…much obliged."

Samantha didn't know when she'd ever been so shaken. She nodded. "Y-you're welcome."

When it was clear that Walter was all right, everyone returned to their post, Samantha included, and the contest continued. To her surprise and delight she made the final round. Hank whooped with triumph, gestured for her to smile wider. Samantha kicked the grin up a notch and resisted the urge to roll her eyes.

Each of the judges came through for another sampling, Walter being more careful this time, then they huddled together to make their final decision. A buzz of anticipation moved through the crowd.

Finally the huddle broke apart. Walter doled out the ribbons and, as each contestant was placed, Samantha grew more and more nervous. Hank's gaze caught hers again and he smiled an endearing, encouraging smile. God, how great it was to have him in her corner, Samantha thought, heartened by that sexy grin. She knew the last thing she should be thinking about right now was a happily-ever-after, because that was nowhere in their immediate future, but oh how she wished it were. How she wished that this contest was over, and that they were locked away in his room—specifically, in his bed—and never had to think about coming out or the consequences of their actions.

Thinking about that bed and Hank brought a whole new host of images to mind, a whole new kind of anticipation racing through her blood. That needy place between her thighs tingled with warmth and her breasts puckered behind the stupid cherry apron she wore. A hum of need buzzed through her entire body and it occurred to Samantha that she didn't know whether she could wait until the contest was over, didn't know if she'd have the patience to get through the rest of this contest when she knew the reward she had coming immediately afterward. How on earth—

"—and first place goes to Samantha Mc-

Cafferty!'' Walter wheezed as loudly into the microphone as his tortured vocal cords would allow.

Startled, Samantha blinked, jerked back into the here and now. What? *First place?* She'd been so caught up in her Hank fantasy, she'd zoned out completely.

"Congratulations, young lady," Walter told her. "You certainly know how to prepare your poultry…and you think quick on your feet," he added, eyes twinkling with warmth.

Hank rushed up behind her, whirled her around and planted a long, hot victory kiss on her lips that ignited an inferno in her already burning loins. His entire body vibrated with excitement and his eyes danced. "That's my girl. I told you that you had it in the bag, didn't I?"

"I—"

"One win down, one to go," Hank told her, ridiculously elated over her chicken victory. That sea-blue gaze glinted with confidence, with the invitation to sin, with untold pleasures she longed to experience. He jerked her forward. "Come on. I'm hungry." The growl in that low sexy baritone left little doubt as to what he was hungry for—and it damn sure wasn't chicken.

He hurried her into the house, walkied Tina and told her that he would unavailable for the next few minutes, then closed the door with a definite click.

"Only a few minutes," Sam teased, though truth

be told she was a smidge disappointed. "I wouldn't have figured you for the quickie type."

Hank stalked toward her. "Who said anything about a quickie?"

Sam frowned. "But I thought—"

"That was your first mistake," he said. He unzipped the dress, then tugged it off her from the shoulder down. "I don't want you to think—I want you to feel." He removed her bra and panties in the same ingenuous fashion, leaving her in nothing but the apron. Her breasts peeked about the top, played hide and seek with the lacy edge. Before she had the time to feel the least bit underdressed, Hank bent and pulled her breast into his hot mouth.

Sam gasped as pleasure arced though her. Her knees turned to jelly, which made the fact that she'd somehow been maneuvered close to the bed all the more fortuitous. She fell backward, bringing him with her. He toyed with the other breast, played at the nipple while he worshipped the other. *Operation Orgasm* indeed, Sam thought dimly. She got it! She finally got it! This had to be one of the most wonderful things that had ever happened to her. The sensation was incredible. No wonder there was power in a woman's cleavage. Clearly Hank loved feeding at her breasts as much as she loved having his hot mouth upon her. She tunneled her fingers in his hair, arched up and pushed her achy breast farther into his mouth. Heat slickened her folds, and she pressed her legs together in a vain attempt to stem the flow of pleasure ebbing through her.

Hank, though, as usual, had other ideas. "These have been quite tasty, however, I'm not…satisfied." And with that loaded statement, he slid down her belly, hooked her legs over his shoulders, then fastened his mouth upon her.

A silent scream formed in the back of her throat and the small of her back bowed from the initial shock of pleasure. Hank lapped at her, flicked his tongue against that sensitive nub nestled at the top of her folds, then slid his finger deep into her channel. The blood beat hotly between her thighs and she tensed, recognizing the heady signal of beginning climax. It was different this time, sharper, keener somehow. The throb built and built, pushed her higher and higher until Sam was sure she'd fly into a million pieces if he didn't stop soon. It was torment and pleasure, a glimpse of heaven in the pit of hell. She bucked beneath him, desperate for him to deliver her there, to lift her up and, just when she thought she couldn't possibly take it anymore, couldn't stand another moment of his wicked torture, her breath caught and lights burst behind her lids, and she quivered from the inside out.

She felt Hank sigh against her. "Mmm. Now that satisfied. For the time being."

He gently disentangled himself from her, then stood. His gaze raked her from head to toe, lingered

on her mouth, breasts, between her legs. Need
shimmered around him and she could tell that every
muscle was locked rigid—particularly one located
directly behind his strained zipper. He winced regretfully. "I hate to do this, but I've got to go. Duty
calls."

Sam nodded, flung an arm over her forehead. She
still hadn't altogether recovered. "I understand." In
fact, she needed to get back on that reservation system. Not that she had any driving need to help him,
but she'd need something to take her mind off—
her gaze drifted over him once more—sex. Or,
more accurately, sex with Hank. She'd had two orgasms since last night, but not one of them had been
with him between her thighs.

Where she wanted him.

And poor Hank hadn't found release yet, an error
she fully intended to rectify as soon as this damned
contest was over.

Hank moved to the door. "I'll see you later." A
promise, Sam noted, not a goodbye. He stopped
short. "Oh, and I got you something. It's, uh, in
the closet."

With that enigmatic statement, he let himself out.

He'd gotten her something? More June Cleaver-
wear flashed through her brain, drawing a wince.
Oh, hell. Intrigued nonetheless, Sam gingerly stood
and made her way to the closet.

Her eyes widened and she clasped her hand to

her mouth. Tears swam before her eyes. "Oh, Hank," she murmured, touched beyond words. Her heart inexplicably swelled and a splash of something wet hit her cheek. He'd always had her heart, Sam thought, but for the first time since she'd truly given it to him, it was at risk because by sharing herself with him, she'd unwittingly given him the power to break it.

Miraculously, at the moment, she simply didn't care.

10

"WHAT IN GOD'S NAME is taking her so long?" Hank demanded. He heaved a long-suffering sigh and glanced at his watch—again. "She's got less than ten minutes before the pageant starts."

Jamie snorted, shrugged. "Hell, you know women. It takes them forever to get ready. They shave, wax and moisturize, paint, curl—" he gestured wearily "—do all sorts of things to themselves. Walking the floor isn't going to make her get ready any faster. You might as well take a load off."

Hank shook his head. He was too keyed-up to sit down. Too impatient. After she'd won the fried chicken and iced tea part of the competition—a coup that, to his unending delight, put her that much closer to moving back here—they'd gone back up to the house and he'd put his head between those delectable thighs and she'd tasted better than he'd ever dreamed. Better than anything he'd ever had in his life. Then, he'd had to go and he'd told her about the dress. Though it was sneaky, he'd lingered outside the door. Had peered through the crack and watched her reaction to his gift.

He'd heard that delighted gasp and something about that sound had made his chest simultaneously lighten and contract. She'd fingered the fine slinky material and her lips had curled with unexpected delight. It had occurred to Hank in that instant that she'd probably had very few unexpected pleasures, surprises, and he'd made a mental note to remedy that problem posthaste. Samantha deserved the best of everything, deserved more than what she'd obviously ever gotten. The dress, he decided, would only be the beginning.

Samantha hadn't come prepared for this pageant like all of the other contestants had, so she'd needed something more formal to wear tonight besides the casual sundress she'd brought along with her. Hank had made a few calls, pulled a few strings and had gotten a boutique in Foley to deliver the kind of dress she needed for this pageant. He'd offered a couple of color suggestions, had given them her size—he'd sneaked a peek at the inside label on a pair of her shorts—then had summed up what he wanted in one word—*sexy.*

The trendy shop hadn't disappointed him.

He couldn't wait to see it on her…then later, *off* of her.

Just thinking about it sent a rush of heat directly to his groin. Made his blood simmer and his palms itch with the need to touch her, to taste her again and again. With effort, Hank banked the need. He didn't have time to think about it now—there'd be time for that later. Right now he needed to focus on this contest, to focus on keeping a level head while he waited for her.

He'd spent the remainder of the afternoon tending to details for their date tonight, then discreetly grilling the secret judges about the contestants and, after careful consideration, abandoned his idea of pulling any strings in her favor—she didn't need them. Samantha was a favored contestant in her own right without his interference.

Still, that hadn't kept him from dropping a few tidbits about her. How she'd sacrificed part of her vacation to help him out this weekend—she'd worked on his reservation system the rest of the afternoon—her generous, selfless nature, all of her endearing little qualities. He hadn't had to embellish or fabricate a single quality—she possessed them all without the artifice.

An unbidden fist of anxiety tightened in his chest. Hank sincerely hoped that she liked what he'd planned for her tonight. He'd pulled out all the stops, had combed his memory for every single detail about her likes and dislikes, and had arranged what he hoped would be her ideal seduction. That's what she'd wanted, after all—to be seduced—what she'd came here for, and he was fully prepared to see that dream to fruition.

If she'd only let him.

With luck tonight's date would be a celebration of many things. A new beginning to an old relationship as well as a victory for her. Hank wanted her to win this pageant for many reasons, the most pressing of which being to get her back here.

He wanted her here.

In Orange Beach.

With him.

Jamie whistled softly and then muttered a low, barely audible, "My God."

Hank stilled. He alternately sensed then smelled her. The fine hairs on his arms stood on end and that tantalizing fruity scent of hers swirled into his nostrils, hot-wired his groin. Hank turned slowly and the site that greeted him sucked all of the air from his lungs, from the very room.

Looking more beautiful than he could have ever imagined, Samantha offered up a soft, tentative smile. "It fits."

Hank couldn't speak, but merely nodded. She was right. It did fit—like a glove. The soft jade color suited her perfectly, matched her eyes, complemented her strawberry-blond curls and brought out the peachy tones of her smooth skin. Hank didn't know much about women's fashion, couldn't begin to describe the cut of her dress, name the fabric or any other such nonsense.

All he knew was that she looked absolutely gorgeous and absolutely, unequivocally *hot.*

The dress showed a lot of cleavage, but still left plenty to the imagination, slithered over her curves and pooled around her ankles. A generous slit started at mid thigh and ended at the hem, revealing just enough leg to make his mouth alternately water, then parch.

She'd anchored her curls in a loose pile on top her head, leaving several stands to whisper over her nape. The style was sexy yet elegant, made a man think about nibbling on that neck while slowly removing the pins from her hair, then feeling it tumble over the backs of his hands. Hank's hands involuntarily fisted.

A pair of rhinestones glittered from her earlobes and a matching necklace circled her neck. The necklace featured a large teardrop stone which lay nestled just above the creamy swell of her breasts. She'd applied her makeup with a dramatic hand, had lined her eyes in dark green, and her lips were painted a luscious raspberry red. When she moved, her skin shimmered with pale golden sparkles. Some sort of body glow, Hank surmised.

Hank finally ended his lengthy perusal and his gaze tangled with hers. He didn't attempt to hide his reaction, couldn't if he'd wanted to—he'd gone instantly—noticeably—hard—and he wanted her to know why. He blinked, gave his head a small imperceptible shake and summed it up in one inarticulate yet wholly accurate word. "Wow."

She let out a small breath and her shoulders wilted with what could only be relief. "Thanks," she murmured. She submitted him to a similar scrutiny and her lips curled ever so slightly. "You look pretty *wow* yourself."

Hank had forgone his typical beach bum uniform and dressed for the evening in a pair of natural linen trousers and a jade silk shirt which he'd purposely chosen because it matched her dress. He lifted his shoulder in a negligent shrug, offered a smile. "I clean up good."

She inclined her head and her eyes twinkled with humor and something else. Heat, Hank realized with a pleased start. "That you do," she said softly.

"You should probably head down to the beach," Jamie said, startling both of them.

Hank had completely forgotten Jamie, a fact his friend had undoubtedly noticed, given the droll tone of his voice.

"Are you ready?" Hank asked her.

Samantha nodded nervously. "As ready as I'll ever be, I suppose."

Hank offered her his arm. He shot her a confident smile. "It's in the bag, baby."

A shallow sigh slipped past her lips. "So you say."

"So I *know*," Hank told her.

And he did. She was unquestionably the most gorgeous woman in this pageant—in the world, as far as he was concerned—and the judges would have to be blind not to see it.

SAMANTHA ALLOWED HANK to walk her down to the sand and, had she not been positively glowing from the look on his face when he'd first seen her, she'd be nervous. As it was, she couldn't be nervous—she was too pleased and frankly, too horny, to think about being nervous.

In fact, were it up to her, she'd just as soon forget about this pageant and skip ahead to their date. Who cared whether those judges thought she was beautiful or not? Samantha thought. The only person whose opinion mattered had already given her incontrovertible proof that she was beautiful to him.

That mouthwatering bulge in Hank's pants had been the only confirmation that she needed. A shiver danced up her spine and her nipples tightened against the flimsy fabric of the dress. She couldn't think about that bulge without thinking about what it meant, what it could do for her and what she'd like to do to it. She couldn't look at Hank without thinking about having that big hard body of his naked and against her own, *inside* her own.

With each second her body became more primed, more desperate for the pleasure she knew she would find in his arms tonight. She'd waited an entire lifetime for this night with Hank and she was heartily impatient to have that happen.

Now.

If he so much as brushed his fingers against her, Samantha knew she'd undoubtedly fall to pieces again, would undoubtedly come. A coil of heat tightened in her womb and she instinctively clenched her feminine muscles to stem the flow of desire. She'd been desperate for release before— had been so desperate in fact that she'd planned this vacation and gone on a damned sex diet—but that was nothing—*nothing*—compared to the way she wanted it now.

Operation Orgasm was in full swing. Her loins had been locked in a fiery pit of hell, her breasts had gone heavy and her poor neglected nipples hadn't once relaxed. She'd careened past ready months ago and now hovered on the edge of sexually frustrated mental illness. Need was a fever in her blood and nothing short of having Hank firmly lodged between her thighs would put an end to it. The two orgasms he'd treated her to thus far had barely taken the edge off. If anything, she was worse now than what she'd been when she'd gotten here. The knowledge was in the power of knowing how he would make her feel. In knowing that he'd delivered her to climax with his fingers, with his mouth, but the grand finale would involve the impressive staff between his thighs—the ultimate orgasm, she knew. He'd been priming her, Sam realized now, purposely denying himself to make tonight the best sex of her life. Another shiver quaked through her at the mere thought. Impatience danced across her nerves. She wanted to get this over with, to be with him.

Frankly—regardless of what Hank thought—the chances of her winning this contest were slim to none, and she couldn't help but think it was a waste of time, couldn't help but wish they could skip it altogether.

Nevertheless, he'd attached a great deal of importance to this pageant, and he'd gone to a lot of trouble to make sure that she had everything she needed for tonight. Samantha couldn't help but be touched. It had been so long since anyone had gone to any trouble on her behalf. The pageant would only last an hour, possibly an hour and a half at best. She could handle it, would use the anticipation to her advantage somehow.

They'd reached the other contestants. Hank bent down and kissed the shell off her ear, causing a flurry of sensation to zigzag through her belly.

"Go get 'em, tiger," Hank murmured, his voice a smooth decadent rumble.

Samantha sucked in a shuddering breath and pushed a smile from her lips, then made her way to behind the long curtain that had been erected behind the makeshift stage. She'd never been in a beauty pageant before and didn't know precisely what was expected of her, other than the fact that she should smile, keep her shoulders drawn back and walk with a modicum of grace. The pageant coordinator had walked them through the ceremony this morning, and she'd explained the program. Basically all Samantha had to remember was to follow the X's.

The stage had been formed into a giant T. Sam had to enter stage left, proceed to X one, pause and smile, then proceed to X two which was located on at the bottom of the T, pause and smile again, then pivot and head to X three. There she would pause and smile again, then exit stage right. Probably, she should just smile the entire time and pray that she didn't do anything embarrassing, like trip on her hem and fall flat on her face. Regrettably, given the wobbly state of her knees, that wasn't out of the realm of possibility.

Mere minutes later, the pageant started. Mayor Flannagin, a portly man with a bad hairpiece but excellent disposition, officiated the festivities.

"Welcome to the first annual *Belle of the Beach*

contest," he told them. He rocked back on his heels and beamed at the audience. "Boy, are you in for a treat," he enthused. "When we decided to host this contest, we sat down and asked ourselves just exactly what makes a Belle. We came up with the following: a Belle is a woman who is gracious, who knows how to prepare fried chicken and iced tea, and a woman who loves her southern heritage and can intelligently answer questions about said history—thus the *Redneck Jeopardy* for our finalists," he added with a wink. "No generic question about world peace for a Belle," he laughed. "In addition, a Belle should be able to sing 'Amazing Grace' and correctly use the old saying, 'bless her heart.' For instance, a Belle might say, 'Eula Mae is dumber than a box of rocks, bless her heart, but she sure can cook a mean pecan pie.'"

The joke drew a laugh from the crowd, and Samantha's lips twitched as well. Mayor Flannagin was right. There was no better way to issue a backhanded compliment than with the old tried and true, fondly uttered *bless her heart.* So long as the heart was duly blessed, the insult wasn't an insult, just an uncharitable observation.

"All right, then," Mayor Flannagin said as the laughter pittered out. "How 'bout we get this show on the road? Before we begin, however, I do want to take just a moment and thank all of our sponsors for making this contest possible—Big Bubba's Ford for donating that shiny new SUV—'' he gestured to a black Expedition, which drew the appropriate awe from the crowd ''—to the Brothers of the Orange Beach for raising the ten grand in cash and to Mitchell's Travel for the trip for two to the Bahamas.'' Mayor Flannagin bounced on the balls of his feet. ''Our crowned Belle this evening will be one lucky girl, indeed.''

She most certainly would, Samantha thought. Would that it could be her. She thought of her ten-year-old car with its slipping transmission and enviously eyed the big sleek SUV. Thought of her modest bank account and imagined adding ten grand to the balance—being able to move back home—then thought of her unstamped passport sitting in the bottom of her purse. She absently chewed her bottom lip.

It really was a tremendous prize package.

Samantha glumly assessed the women around her. And these *really* were beautiful women. No matter how good Hank thought she looked, those judges hadn't been around her enough to be affected by the sex diet—by her elevated pheromones—and she knew she didn't have a prayer of duping them with it the way she had Hank.

Her heart squeezed at the sudden uncharitable insight, causing her to suck in a small breath. She really had duped him, hadn't she? Samantha thought with a start. When she'd first thought of using this diet to snag a man for the week, Samantha had never considered the duplicity of the act. Had never given much thought to the fact that she was essentially tricking a man into intimacy with her.

But now she did and the idea didn't sit well with her at all. Granted, she was tricking them into sex—her lips curled wryly—a pastime men unequivocally enjoyed, so really what was the harm?

There hadn't been, Samantha realized, until she'd miraculously snared Hank with her mantrap pheromones.

Now she felt like a cheat, felt sneaky. She should come clean, Samantha thought abruptly. She should tell Hank about the diet, about the pheromones and just admit the truth. He'd be outraged, of course, would probably try to deny that the pheromones had anything to do with why he'd suddenly admitted to wanting her, but Samantha knew better. He might have felt something for her—might have wanted her—but if she hadn't gone on this sex diet, he most likely would have never acted on the attraction. After all, he'd kept it hidden for years.

Sam blew out a breath. But she wouldn't tell him the truth. She was too weak, too far gone and too in love with him to even consider not taking what he'd offered.

Hank wanted her—truly wanted her—and she didn't care if her sex diet had made him admit it.

Should she care? Probably. But she'd rather have this stolen week, than not have him at all. Pathetic? Yes. But she simply couldn't help herself. She'd been in love with Hank for as long as she could remember, had dreamed that he'd one day look at her the way he had tonight. Like he'd wanted to eat her up—like he'd done today, Sam thought, going warm again. Like he couldn't wait to have her.

She might not be doing the right thing for the long term, but she knew she was doing the right thing for the moment.

For this brief little portion of time, Hank Masterson would be hers. She'd deal with the residual effects of her decision later—no doubt that would involve a considerable amount of heartache and tears—but, again, that was a price she'd gladly pay. A small smile quirked her lips. This night with Hank wouldn't come cheap, she knew—she was essentially charging it on a Heartbreak Visa—but how could she refuse? How could she not go through with it when Hank had offered her everything she'd ever wanted?

Him.

She simply couldn't resist.

Her gaze was inexplicably drawn to where he sat. Jamie had taken the seat next to him, and though he was a handsome devil, Samantha knew she'd have never been able to go through with her original plan. She only wanted one man—Hank—and no other would ever suffice. Tonight he looked particularly wonderful.

His pale blond hair had been carefully smoothed into place, though the breeze was wreaking havoc with his style. He wore a jade green shirt open at the throat and a pair of natural linen slacks that showcased that narrow-hipped swagger and tight little ass. Honestly, the man had a rear that made a woman fantasize about sinking her teeth into it. Tight and curved just so. A designer watch was fastened around his tanned wrist and he wore a pair of casual leather Dockers on his feet. His teeth flashed white against his tanned skin as he smiled at something Jamie said, sending a rush of sweet emotion into Samantha's chest.

As though he could feel her stare, Hank suddenly looked up and caught her gaze. He smiled reassuringly and gave her an encouraging thumbs-up. Samantha returned the grin and, with effort, tuned back into the pageant. The line had started to move and she slowly made her way toward the stage. Just get it over with, Samantha thought as her belly clenched with resigned anxiety. That was all. Hank was waiting for her, and as soon as this was over, she'd be with him.

"Contestant number twenty-seven, Samantha McCafferty!"

Samantha summoned a bright smile and took the stage.

"Samantha's a dietician originally from Orange Beach though she currently makes her home in Aspen, Colorado. Her hobbies include attending Civil War Reenactments, visiting historic battlegrounds and volunteering at her local nursing home."

What? Samantha thought wildly. Her smile froze. She hadn't written any of that stuff! She'd never been to a Civil War Reenactment in her life! Her gaze cut to Hank, who looked incredibly pleased with himself and this time offered a double thumbs-up. She'd break his thumbs, Samantha decided ominously.

Right after she slept with him.

"Samantha's favorite song is Hank Williams Jr.'s 'If Heaven Ain't a Lot Like Dixie' and she enjoys quilting." Mayor Flannagin smiled approvingly. "All Belle qualities, indeed."

By this time, Samantha had made it to the end of the runway, where she smiled for five seconds, then backtracked and made her way to the last X. She manufactured her most winsome smile, then swiftly exited the stage. She peeked around the curtain, caught Hank's eye, and furiously motioned for him to come to her.

Hank was beaming when he reached her side. "You were *fantastic*. I swear, you looked ab—"

Samantha poked him in the chest. "You tampered with my entry!" she snarled. "How could you do that? *Why* would you do that?"

Hank flushed guiltily. "I read over your entry form and decided it could use a little, er, spiffing up."

"Spiffing up?"

"Yeah. Reading a good book or exercising might work for another pageant—" his dubious expression said that he doubted the credibility of that remark "—but this is a *Belle* pageant and you needed something more…fitting."

"Hank, you lied," Samantha whispered, outraged. "I've never been to a Civil War Reenactment in my life," she hissed angrily, "and I damn sure don't know how to quilt." Hell, she could barely replace a button. "What on earth possessed you to do such a thing?"

"I want you to win," he said, looking truly—adorably—baffled, as though this settled everything. "I want you to move back here."

Leave it to Hank to sum things up so succinctly, Samantha thought as her rightful irritation fled at his honest, heart-warming reply. "Well, thank you. I appreciate it," she told him, somewhat mollified. Still… "You haven't done anything else I should know about have you?"

Though he didn't necessarily pause before he shook his head, Samantha felt it all the same. Her eyes narrowed. "Hank," she said warningly.

He hastily kissed her on the cheek, then straightened. "They're about to announce the finalists. I'd better go.'' He turned and fled before she could find out anything more.

''Dammit, Hank!'' Samantha growled.

The music cued once more and Samantha turned and slid back into line. Hank was right. They were ready to announce the finalists. Though an ominous feeling had settled in her gut—she couldn't help but be filled with dread, couldn't help but worry about what else Hank had done to ''help'' her win—Samantha nonetheless pasted a smile on her face and returned to the stage.

''Our judges have chosen tonight's finalists,'' Mayor Flannagin announced with proper fanfare. He shook the little envelope meaningfully. ''All right then... In no particular order, our finalists are...Tammy Nichols, Kim Patterson, Sophie Jenkins—''

Samantha's belly flip-flopped and she resisted the urge to wring her hands. She knew she didn't stand a chance, but still some vain part of her wanted to be wrong.

''—Chloe Waters, Lauren Walker, Annette Davies, Lucy Hartman—''

Hank would be so disappointed if she didn't at least make the final after all the trouble he'd gone to on her behalf. She wanted to final for him, not for herself. She wasn't that shallow. Looks weren't everything, despite the effort she'd put into being pretty. She knew that and yet...

"—Lori Horn, Leslie Fowler—"

Her shoulders sagged, certain that the last name called wouldn't be hers. Who cared? Samantha told herself, fighting bitter disappointment. One of these women might win this contest, but she'd be leaving with Hank. That was better than any prize package anyone could ever give her. That was better than—

"—and Samantha McCafferty!" Mayor Flannagin announced happily.

There was a two-second delay between her ears and her brain, and in that two seconds, Samantha's quivering stomach dropped to her knees and Hank vaulted from his seat and whooped like a madman. *She was a finalist. Her*—a finalist. Samantha couldn't believe it. Couldn't make the realization sink in.

"I'd like to thank all of our contestants. Aren't they beautiful, folks?" Mayor Flannagin said, gesturing to all of the contestants. "Just gorgeous. Now, finalists, if you'll all step forward, we'll ready ourselves for *Redneck Jeopardy*. Why?" he joked and wraggled his brows meaningfully. "Because there's more to being a Belle than a pretty face."

Samantha had worn a fake smile for the entire evening, but the one currently stretched across her face was genuine. Out of all these gorgeous women, those judges had decided that she had some special quality that put her above the rest. *Her*. A light, warm tingly feeling moved through her chest.

Samantha's gaze found Hank's once more. That sea-blue gaze glittered with equal parts happiness and pride, and he was still clapping wildly. He winked at her again, gave her a thumbs-up and mouthed, ''It's in the bag.''

She didn't know about that, Samantha thought, but for the first time this evening, she didn't feel like she'd been wasting her time. In fact, she felt pretty damned good…right up until a telltale itch started at her wrist and quickly spread to her elbow.

Oh, hell, Samantha thought as panic punched her dread level into the red zone. She felt her smile turn pained.

Her damned antihistamine was wearing off.

11

OH HELL, HANK THOUGHT as he watched Samantha
surreptitiously scratch her wrist, watched her smile
momentarily freeze. He knew that look. She was at
it again—scratching. He frowned. Mosquitoes, hell.
Something else was at work here.

He knew it.

Samantha had never been a good liar and she'd
looked entirely—unaccountably—guilty too many
times in recent memory for comfort. Hank paused
to consider her as that nagging inkling played hide-
and-seek in his brain again. It was an important
thought and for the life of him, he couldn't catch
it, couldn't figure out what he was undoubtedly
missing.

But what the hell could it be? he wondered. As
far as he knew, she'd never kept a secret from him.
Other than the fact that she'd never had an orgasm—an injustice he'd already rectified, by God—
and even then she'd finally shared that with him.
So what could it be? A horrible thought surfaced—
could she be sick?—but he dismissed the idea almost in the same instant. Samantha was the picture

of health, had never looked better in her life. No, Hank thought consideringly. That wasn't it…but as soon as this pageant was over, he fully intended to find out just exactly what was going on.

Right now, however, a more pressing thought took hold—she'd made it to the finals. A smile inexplicably claimed his lips and a curious mixture of joy and pride moved into his chest, forcing him to expel a deep, satisfied breath.

Hank had watched her face throughout the entire process, had watched the nervousness and anxiety dampen her nevertheless hopeful gaze. She'd pretended that this pageant hadn't meant anything to her, but Hank knew better. She didn't want to care—but she did.

Samantha had self-preservation down to an art form, kept her expectations low in order to stem possible disappointment. How sad, Hank thought, that she couldn't invest in the one emotion that everyone else took for granted—hope. He sighed. Another injustice that needed rectifying, and just one of many that he planned to correct.

If she had any idea just how beautiful she was she wouldn't hesitate to hope. Hank let his gaze linger on her for a moment, took in the slim yet curvy line of her body, that gorgeous face and those oh-so-tempting lips. Lust detonated in his loins, instantly pushing his rod up like a rocket awaiting a three-two-one countdown. Just the memory of kissing her, of sampling those lips—and other tasty areas—made him want to snag her hand, haul her around back and take her hard and fast against the stage. A small smile rolled around his lips.

Not exactly in keeping with the lengthy seduction he had planned for tonight, but what the hell? Men were animals, himself included. He just wanted her—had wanted her forever, for pity's sake—and the sooner the better.

She wanted him, too, thank God, Hank thought, vastly relieved. She might not be sure of the outcome of this hellish attraction, might have reservations about it, but she wanted him all the same. Those pale green eyes had glittered with something more than anxiety a few moments ago—they'd glittered with pure, unadulterated lust. Hank had formed the mistaken impression that Samantha couldn't get any sexier.

He'd been wrong—Samantha turned on was lethally sexy.

"Whose idea was the *Redneck Jeopardy?*" Jamie asked from the side of his mouth, drawing Hank's thoughts north of his groin.

Ten small lecterns on casters—which had been emblazoned with the *Redneck Jeopardy* logo—were rolled out and put in front of each contestant. Mayor Flannagin was presently doling out buzzers. If he got any happier, Hank thought, their portly little civil servant would undoubtedly burst.

Hank resisted the urge to roll his eyes and blew out a breath. "Hell, who do you think? Mayor Flannagin. Said he wanted something 'different.'"

Jamie snorted. "It's different, all right. How do you think Samantha will fare?"

"Well," Hank said with a succinct nod. "She's sharp as a tack." And she was. Samantha could converse intelligently about any given subject and had always been a trivia buff. The oddest, most insignificant little factoids stuck to her brain like flypaper, and the more bizarre the better. Hank was sure she'd rather play *Redneck Jeopardy* than answer a question. He caught her eye, frowned while he watched her covertly claw at a place on her arm. She flushed and immediately looked away.

"What's with the scratching?" Jamie asked, noticing her peculiar behavior as well.

"I don't know," Hank said slowly. "She keeps scratching. She's done it off and on since she got here."

Jamie hummed under his breath. "Looks like she might be having an—"

Whatever Jamie had intended to say was cut off as Mayor Flannagin thumped his microphone to get everyone's attention.

"Okay, ladies and gentlemen, it's time to begin." The genuine *Jeopardy* tune began. "Each of our contestants have been given a buzzer and the rules have been explained. They're simple, really.

Buzz if you know the answer, and each answer must be phrased in the form of a question." He gestured to Mrs. Flannagin, who sat at a small table toward the edge of the stage. "My lovely wife will be keeping score. The first contestant to successfully answer five questions will be crowned our winner." He glanced at the finalists. "Ready, ladies?"

A combination of murmured assents and nods moved down the line, Samantha's among them. Hank watched her pull in a bolstering breath and then absently rub the elbow on her other arm. He frowned again. What the hell was—

"Here we go... According to the *Farmer's Almanac,* when is the best time to wean a calf?"

To Hank's immediate satisfaction, Samantha buzzed in first. "What is, when the signs are below the knees?"

Mayor Flannagin grinned. "Correct. Question number two... According to Forrest Gump, life is like what?"

Samantha hit her buzzer, but a mere nanosecond too late. Another finalist, a petite busty blonde with a tan like seasoned leather, beat her to the punch. "What is a box of chocolates?"

"Correct." He beamed. "Smart ladies we've got here folks, smart ladies." He sighed. "Okay...what legendary southern belle swore that, as God as her witness, she'd never go hungry again?"

There was a flurry of movement and startled gasps as every finalist knew the answer to that question. Thankfully Samantha was quicker with the finger and that no-brainer went to her.

"Who is Scarlett O'Hara," she said. She reached down and rubbed the back of her thigh.

Okay, Hank thought. Two down, three to go. He leaned forward.

Mayor Flannagin cleared his throat. "How many pecks are in a bushel?"

Samantha again. "What is four?"

Pleased, Hank elbowed Jamie in the side. "What'd I tell you?" he whispered. "She's sharp."

Jamie nodded, but didn't speak. Tension tightened the back of Hank's neck as he shifted closer. He'd known that she could win this contest—had never doubted it—but, aside from admitting to her that he wanted her, watching her do it had to be one of the most nerve-racking things he'd ever done. His damned stomach was practically in knots.

"What's the snack of choice with an RC Cola?"

Samantha's buzzer sounded first. "What is a Moon Pie?"

"Correct again, Samantha," Mayor Flannagin told her, his face wreathed with a smile. "If my calculations are correct, Ms. McCafferty is one point away from being crowned our first *Belle of the Beach* and as such, will go home with our grand prize package.'' Quiet anticipation moved through the crowd as he studied the next question.

Hank had scooted to the edge of his seat. He stared at Samantha, silently willing her to look in his direction, and was rewarded when she finally found his gaze. She wore a hopeful, nervous smile that was just vulnerable enough to make him wish that he could storm the stage and kiss her. He gave her an encouraging grin and made a lazy slam dunk gesture that edged up her wobbly smile.

''Quite possibly for the win,'' Mayor Flannagin announced with the appropriate amount of gravity and enthusiasm, ''what substance is used to season a cast-iron skillet?''

The sound of sharp inhaled breaths echoed through the contestants and crowd. Any southern cook worth her salt knew the answer to that question. Hank all but vaulted from his seat in an effort to find out who buzzed in first, and to his abject disappointment soon realized that it wasn't Samantha. It was the petite blonde with the leather tan again, Samantha's only real competition in this category.

''Shortening,'' she said.

Mayor Flannagin winced regretfully. ''Sorry, darlin'. You forgot to phrase it in the form of a question.''

His thoughts exactly, Hank thought, and settled back down once more. Jesus, this was maddening.

He speared his hands through his hair. Tension crawled up his back. She was one away from winning, one measly question away from being able to move back here, one measly question away from the end of this contest. Which put him mere minutes away from each and every one of his desires. His desire to see her win, his desire to have her back in Orange Beach, and his desire to root himself firmly between her thighs.

"Ms. McCafferty buzzed in second, so the question goes to her." He paused dramatically. "Samantha, for the win...what substance is used to season a cast-iron skillet?"

Hank's gaze swung back to Samantha who wore a disbelieving absolute smile of delight. She swallowed, scratched the inside of her wrist and said in a somewhat small voice, "What is shortening?"

"Correct!" Mayor Flannagin boomed. Hank sprang from his seat and cheered wildly. She'd done it! She'd won! Beside him, the normally sedate Jamie had also vaulted from his seat. "Ladies and gentlemen, it is my great pleasure to present our very first *Belle of the Beach*...Samantha McCafferty!"

Samantha's expression wavered between thrilled and astonished, but the smile she wore was absolutely blinding in its beauty. Lynyrd Skynyrd's "Sweet Home Alabama" intro launched from the speakers but was barely audible above the roar of applause and catcalls from the crowd. Mrs. Flannagin hurried forward and placed a sparkling rhinestone crown on Samantha's head.

It was in that moment that her misty green gaze inexplicably slammed into his, rooting him to the sand where he stood. Hank's breath left him in a quiet whoosh and he found himself sucked into a vacuum, away from the din, from the noise—from everything but her. Some unnamed emotion winged through his chest, tripped his heart rate into overdrive. His palms tingled, his throat tightened and for all intents and purposes the rest of the world simply receded, faded into insignificance. Which seemed disconcertingly appropriate because *she* was the most significant thing that had ever happened to him.

That frighteningly clear realization jolted him and he blinked, breaking the special connection. Seemingly startled as well, Sam blinked and turned her attention to Mayor Flannagin who was enthusiastically pressing a set of keys into her hand while Mrs. Flannagin presented her with the prize check and vacation voucher.

Mayor Flannagin enthusiastically nudged Samantha forward, presenting her to the still-riotous crowd. "Our Belle," he said appreciatively.

No, Hank silently amended—*his* belle.

Starting tonight.

"YOU COULD HAVE DRIVEN, you know."

Samantha settled back against the cool leather interior of her new SUV, closed her eyes and sighed softly. "I know...but since I don't know where we're going, what would be the point?"

"It's called a *surprise*, Sam," Hank said drolly.

Samantha grinned, rolled her head toward Hank and peered at him through the darkness. The dash lights illuminated the smooth planes of his profile, the thin blade of his nose, the sharp angle of his jaw. She bit her lip as need ballooned below her navel, muddling her insides. Just looking at him made her warm and wet, made her heart pound and her blood simmer. God, she was a hopeless case.

Yes, she'd just won a beauty pageant—a feat she'd never in a million years would have anticipated. The resulting euphoria from that unexpected victory still glowed happily inside her.

And, yes, she'd just won ten grand, a new SUV and a vacation—all unequivocally wonderful by anyone's standards—and yet the joy of the windfall paled in comparison when compared to the vast relief she felt now that the damned contest was over and she could claim her real prize—Hank.

She'd waited so very long—her entire life—for this night with him, and though she still had reservations about what they were about to do, she wouldn't dare change her mind. While Hank would undoubtedly regret things later—once he was out from under the influence of her *über*pheromones, Samantha thought with no small amount of dreaded anticipation—she nonetheless knew that she would never regret being with him. How could she when every breath she breathed seemed tied to this night? To the coming moments? When every single cell in her body sang with desperate expectation?

Sam's gaze turned inward as she relived that bizarre moment when their gazes had connected right after they'd crowned her *Belle of the Beach.* Hank had been thrilled for her—she'd read that immediately in the wide triumphant smile stretched across his tanned, handsome face. But there had been something more…something that had simultaneously thrilled and terrified her. Something beyond sexual attraction or mere friendly affection.

He'd been annoyingly secretive about where they were going and his plans for tonight. Oh, she knew what he had planned, could tell from the heat in those sea-blue eyes that she would undoubtedly find herself thoroughly seduced by the end of the evening.

And she couldn't wait. Every feminine part of her yearned for him, was throbbingly aware of him.

But it was what he'd concocted which led up to that ultimate seduction that had her nerves twitching with raw anticipation. He'd been gone the majority of the day, and he was endearingly nervous, which led her to believe that he'd gone to a lot of trouble to plan their evening. She knew beyond a shadow of a doubt that he wouldn't be nervous about making love to her—that smoldering gaze he'd been treating her to exuded as much heat as confidence, an arousing combination to be sure.

Furthermore, he hadn't even wanted to give her time to change after the pageant, had tried to herd her speedily into the SUV and be off. Sam would have liked nothing better herself, but had insisted upon changing first so that she could sneak an antihistamine. The damned things were wearing off entirely too fast. She made a mental note to double up on her next dose because she fully intended to increase her sex diet portions, triple them if need be. Extreme? Yes. But she couldn't afford not to.

Now that she finally had Hank, she didn't dare run the risk of losing her pheromone advantage. At least not until this week was over. Just the idea of it being over cast a pall over her heart, so she firmly closed the door on that line of thinking. She didn't have much time left and she had absolutely no intention of letting an inevitable conclusion ruin what would undoubtedly be the best time of her life. She wanted this memory preserved unblemished. She'd treasure it forever, would pull it out on lonely nights and mull it over like a care-worn photograph.

Hank wheeled the SUV off the road and aimed it down a long, winding packed-sand drive. After a moment, he slowed to a stop. ''We'll have to walk from here," he told her. He leaned over the console and treated her to a slow but thorough kiss, a prelude to the night ahead, and by the time he reluctantly dragged his lips from hers, Samantha would have gladly forgone any elaborate seduction, would have been just as happy if he'd asked her to crawl into the back seat. Her muscles had melted with pleasure and a steady throbbing heat had commenced in her nipples and between her thighs.

She swallowed a sigh, then opened the door and forced her wobbly legs to make the trek to the back of the SUV where Hank presently stood. He hauled a picnic basket and a flashlight out of the cargo area, shut the door and then turned to face her. "It's just a short walk."

Sam nodded and followed him, anticipation dogging her every step. Her palms tingled and gooseflesh suddenly erupted all over her body. Every article she'd read about sex, every how-to-please-a-lover manual, every single carnal act of depravity she'd ever fantasized about had hastened to the forefront of her mind. Her ultimate dream—sex with Hank—was just within her reach and the very idea made her so hot that self-combustion became a genuine fear. She shook herself, dragged in a shallow breath and tried to concentrate on something besides sex with Hank. And more sex with Hank. And even more sex with Hank.

Sam frowned thoughtfully. Like where they were.

Though she was fairly familiar with her hometown, she didn't have any idea where they were. At least, not precisely. Hank had taken Fort Morgan Road, had driven past several new condominium complexes and private subdivisions, but she hadn't been paying close enough attention to discern their exact location. A cloud moved past the moon briefly illuminating her companion. Her gaze drifted over his broad shoulders, down the masculine line of his back and settled on his delectable ass. Sam's lips curled as an arrow of heat landed another bull's-eye in her belly. Her mind had been on other things.

Hank threw her a look over his shoulder. "Watch your step. There's a bit of an incline."

Samantha followed him up a steep dune, was slightly winded as they reached the top...and her breath left her altogether at the sight that greeted her.

She stopped, stunned, unable to move.

Hank had half-descended the sandy hill before he realized that she hadn't followed him. An endearing, slightly relieved grin toyed with his oh-so-sexy lips as he noted her flabbergasted expression. "I take it the lady is impressed," he said sardonically. She didn't have to see those sinful blue eyes to know that a twinkle of amusement undoubtedly danced in their depths.

Sam swallowed tightly. *Impressed* couldn't begin to describe the maelstrom of emotions currently churning in her rapidly beating heart, a heart that had all but stopped just a moment ago in shocked delight. "How did you— When did you—" She gestured helplessly, unable to finish as her gaze took in the sight from the top of the dune.

A huge steep-pitched tent straight out of an Arabian fantasy had been erected on the deserted sand. Yards and yards of gauzy jewel-colored fabrics billowed in the soft breeze. A curving pathway of luminary candles invited one across the sand, and outlined their outdoor boudoir. Big tropical plants anchored each corner of the makeshift room and hundreds—*hundreds*—of candles danced in the warm night air.

An intimate table set for two draped with crisp white linens and a bouquet of hot pink oleander as well as a silver champagne bucket completed the romantic setting. Someone, Hank she imagined, had dug a fire pit and a merry flame flickered from the ground, adding even more ambiance to the romantically whimsical decor.

Hank set the picnic basket next to the table, and she watched his body become a shadow as he disappeared into the tent. He bent over and a mere second later Barry White's smooth, deep voice resonated softly from inside the virtually see-through structure.

An inexplicable grin tilted her lips.

Hank emerged from the tent and flashed her a smile. "Mood music," he told her.

Like she needed it, Sam thought with a derisive snort. "Looks like you've thought of everything," she said instead. Of their own volition, her feet had finally begun the descent down the dune. She simply couldn't believe that he'd done all of this for her, that he'd taken the time to pull something like this together just for *her*.

And he'd definitely done it for her.

Samantha knew Hank would have been just as happy to have made love to her back in his room at the B&B—hell, he'd been ready to make love to her in the damned kitchen, and only moments ago she would have gladly done it in the back seat of her new SUV—but he'd wanted something special for her—something unforgettable—and he'd most definitely achieved that.

Making love with Hank could never be an unforgettable experience, she knew—God, how she knew!—but he'd gone the extra mile, had even incorporated some of her favorite things—oleander, candlelight and champagne—and only someone with a hard heart would fail to be touched. Considering he unwittingly owned her heart, the gesture was almost too wonderful to bear. Too much. Sam swallowed tightly.

The tent in and of itself was simply unbelievable. She cast a covert peek inside catching a glimpse at dozens of satin floor pillows piled on top of the sand. An image of what they would be doing on those pillows in just a short while flashed before her eyes and a bolt of heat ignited in her belly at the mere thought.

Candles in jeweled votives had been suspended from the interior poles in varying heights, giving the fanciful impression of multicolored stars. The combined textures and colors, the silky satin, sensual jewel tones and the warm glow of candlelight was a feast for the senses. Inspired images of hot bodies and bare skin, of erotic fantasies and hard orgasms. Sam expelled a soft shuddering breath.

She couldn't imagine anything more perfect than what he'd created. Couldn't imagine anything more beautiful, more romantic. Something sweet and tender swelled in her chest, pushed into her throat and misted her eyes. She blinked it away, refusing to acknowledge the sentiment. There would be time for that later.

Hank, who stood by the table and who clearly couldn't stand to wait for her response any longer looked at her and said, "Well?"

The hint of anxiety in his voice ridiculously

warmed her heart. He wanted her approval, her opinion, her reaction.

Her.

"It's utterly incredible," she finally managed with a choked laugh. "I'm speechless. I, uh—" She looked around, unable to frame the right reply. "I don't know what to say."

"How about 'Thank you, Hank'?" he suggested with a wry smile, lightening the curiously tense moment.

Sam chuckled softly. "I suppose that would work. Thank you, Hank," she dutifully repeated.

"You're welcome." He'd filled a flute and handed it to her. "Are you hungry?"

She had been right up until this very minute...but one hunger had superceded another. Sam bit her lip as another rush of wanton heat engulfed her and she slid him a glance. She let her gaze lingeringly roam from one end of his body to the other, then finally met his gaze. She expelled a soft sigh. "Not really. Are you?"

Hank had grown unnaturally still, evidence that he'd sensed her abrupt change in mood. His lips curled ever so slightly and a wicked glint reflected in his suddenly heavy-lidded gaze. "I could eat—"

Sam swallowed a disappointed sigh. Now he wanted to wait? They'd waited all this time and he couldn't forgo a single meal to—

"—you."

Sam's mental tirade came to a grinding halt as the *you* surfaced amidst the irritation and she, too, stilled. Her gaze tangled with his and her fertile imagination instantly imagined his head once again between her legs, making a feast of her. Warmth rushed to her core, slickened her feminine folds. Oh, thank God, she thought.

Finally.

Then, though her stomach clenched with nervous anticipation, Sam set her glass aside, tentatively leaned forward and kissed Hank. The moment her lips touched his, every hesitation, every vestige of nervous anticipation vanished, washed away by years of unrequited lust and longing. She funneled every ounce of desire, of sexual promise, she could muster into the melding of their mouths, then only after the briefest hesitation, boldly slid her hand over his groin.

His startled wince of pleasure hissed through her blood, validating the brash move. "Okay," she told him as she drew back. "But I'll need to inspect your…utensil…first."

With an exaggerated swing of her hips, she turned and made her way toward the tent.

12

SHE'D BARELY HAD TIME TO BEMOAN her use of metaphor before a broken chuckle erupted from Hank's throat and she sensed a flurry of movement from behind her.

"I'll show you a utensil," he warned with a choked laugh, then with a running leap, lightly tackled her from behind.

Sam gave a startled yelp, which quickly turned into a squeal of laughter as they landed with a soft *oomph* on top of the pillows.

Still laughing, Hank rolled her underneath him and nuzzled her neck. His warm weight engulfed her, causing a sensual heat to sparkle like stardust from the tips of her toes to the top of her head. Gooseflesh peppered her arms, raced down her spine. She was seconds away from completing *Operation Orgasm*—of reaching her ultimate goal— and the fact that Hank would be the man to see her to that place was the crowning glory of that coup.

Impatience spiked. Now that the time was at hand, she didn't want to wait another second— hadn't she waited long enough? She no longer desired a grand seduction. She only had one single-minded desire—to feel his naked skin beneath her palms, feel the long, hard length of him embedded deeply inside of her.

In short, she wanted him—*now*.

Sam eagerly tugged his shirt from his waistband, felt a smile bloom on her lips as she slid her hands up the sleek skin at the small of his back. God, he felt wonderful.

Hot, hard and thrilling.

He shuddered beneath her touch, giving her irrefutable proof that the fever that burned inside her burned in him as well.

He emitted a low growl of approval, then left her ear and found her mouth once more. The kiss was slow and deep, thorough and inexplicably drugging. His tongue skillfully probed her mouth, curled around her own, then explored the sensitive recesses hidden behind her bottom lip. He fed at her mouth, purposefully baiting a hunger that needed no provocation.

A rush of heat flooded her womb, drenched her sex; her limbs grew heavy and a hot sluggish warmth slid through her veins. Every cell in her body was mad for release and he'd put her in this frenzied state of desperation with a mere kiss. If it didn't feel so damned wonderful, she'd be annoyed. As it was, who could be annoyed? Who would bother?

Particularly since one of Hank's hands had commenced with a similar exploration as her own.

She felt a gentle tug at the hem of her blouse, then the brush of his warm fingers against her belly. She sucked in a stuttered breath, causing her abdomen to quiver beneath his lazy yet determined touch. His palm skimmed her rib cage, trekked slowly—tantalizingly—upward until his hand grazed the underside of her pouting breast. Her nipple contracted, hardened in anticipation of his touch.

Sam shifted, pushing her aching breast into his hand, and a slow sigh escaped as his thumb rasped over the tightened peak. She'd adopted a *why bother?* attitude and foregone the bra. And thank God, Sam thought as her eyes all but rolled back in her again. The sensation was amazing, had validated every ounce of shellfish she'd eaten, made every antihistamine worthwhile.

And, strictly speaking, they hadn't even reached the good part yet.

Hank's masculine purr of pleasure reverberated in their joined mouths. She greedily ate that sound, hungered for more like it. An inexplicable flash of heat ignited in her womb, singeing her frayed nerve endings.

"God, Sam, you smell so good," he growled, his voice deep and sexy.

So did he, Samantha thought, inhaling his particular scent. Beach and Man. Irresistible. Intoxicating.

And he'd probably smell better naked.

She tugged at his shirt again, impatiently this time, drawing a wicked chuckle from Hank. He drew back and allowed her to pull the silky garment over his head. Though she'd been privy to Hank's chest countless times, this was the first opportunity she'd ever had to view the impressive landscape with such close scrutiny, the first chance she'd had to admire the absolute manly perfection of his body. His skin gleamed like polished bronze in the candlelight and the muscles bunched and flexed with a lazy yet powerful grace.

Mesmerized, Sam slid her hands over the sleek, supple landscape, over the bumpy ridges of his abdomen, felt his pale, feathery, masculine hair abrade her palms as she smoothed them farther still over his pecs and onto his powerful shoulders. Her body vibrated with insistent need and her very insides seemed to melt with a wanton heat. She leaned forward and licked the hollow of his throat, savored the salty flavor of his skin.

Hank took advantage of her raised position and, when she drew back, dragged her shirt off as well. Those sea-blue eyes darkened to the hue of the sky before an approaching storm, grew heavy-lidded and hot as he gazed at her nearly naked form.

He wanted her.

Confidence bubbled up through her, weighted her shoulders and, with a small smile and a delicate arch of her back, she sank against the pillows. Hank swiftly followed her. To her supreme relief, he didn't dally with soft seductive touches—which she would have unquestionably enjoyed—but eagerly shaped his hands to her achy breasts, then fastened his hot mouth upon one.

He must have read her mind, because at this precise moment—when need had all but become a living, breathing thing writhing in the pit of her belly—she most definitely preferred the direct approach.

Sam's breath left her in a startled whoosh of pleasure. A bolt of sheer joy arrowed directly to her womb, then mushroomed through her.

He suckled greedily, flattened the rosy peak against the roof of his mouth, then licked and nipped and generally worshipped her until she could scarcely draw a breath. She arched up, urging him to further feast upon her, shamelessly begging him for this desperate pleasure and more.

Between the cool silk at her back, his big hard body above her and his hot mouth upon her breast, Sam was literally burning up from the inside out. Suddenly all those hedonistic, depraved scenarios she'd fantasized and imagined faded into insignificance. There was nothing more carnal—more seductive—than having him like this. Wanting her as much as she wanted him. Desperate, as she was.

She whimpered as he continued his mind-numbing assault. A hot throb commenced between her thighs, frantically beating to some primal genetically programmed beat. She instinctively tilted her hips toward his, clenched her feminine muscles and felt another rush of liquid heat coat her folds, seep into her panties. She squirmed against him.

She wanted—

She needed—

Hank chuckled against her, his warm breath breezing across her bare nipple. "Calm down," he told her. "Can't you see that I'm trying to seduce you?"

No, she couldn't see—she was cross-eyed with lust. A proverbial bitch in heat without the slightest notion of shame or propriety. Hank made a slow lazy lap around her breast with his tongue. She bit her lip as the pleasure eddied through her.

Then again, pride and dignity wouldn't give her the orgasm she so desperately wanted.

"I'm seduced," Sam all but growled. "Take off your clothes. Or more important, take off mine."

Another sexy laugh rumbled from his chest. "I think I'll know when you're ready," he said infuriatingly. "But I agree. We should definitely get naked." His hand slid down her belly and deftly unbuttoned her shorts. "You go first."

She shivered to the tune of her zipper, then lifted her hips to further accommodate him. Hank slung her shorts off to the side, then hooked a single finger beneath the lacy edge of her panties. His eyes darkened. "Nice," he murmured, rubbing the silky fabric. He gave a gentle tug and discarded them in the same careless fashion, and then blew out a halting breath as he gazed at her. If the look he'd given her before was hungry, then the one he was treating her to now could only be described as *ravenous*.

Hank dipped his fingers past her curls, dragged them through her drenched folds—effectively snatching the very breath from her lungs—then, in an act more erotic than she could have ever imagined, his gaze tangled with hers and he inserted those same fingers into his mouth and slowly—purposefully—licked them clean.

Sam almost had an immaculate orgasm.

"But that's nicer," he told her, eyes gleaming with somnolent wickedness.

She'd say, thought Sam. But before she could say anything, Hank positioned himself between her legs, spread her thighs and coupled his mouth to her sex.

Though she would have thought that she'd be prepared for it this time, the sheer shock of sensation rent a silent gasp of delight from her and once again bowed her body from the pillows. Her head rolled to the side and she closed her eyes tightly, trembling as pleasure bolted through her. Sweet Jesus. She'd never dreamed— Never imagined—

A low growl of pleasure rose from Hank's throat as he licked and suckled at her. He slid his tongue deep inside her, then moved forward and fastened his mouth upon that tiny sensitized nub nestled beneath her curls. Sam whimpered as sensation, dark and sweet, sluiced through her, and she shamelessly tilted her hips against him, silently begging for more of the same hedonistic torture. He eagerly sucked, then blew lightly against her, licked her long and slow, then hard and deep.

She felt it then, the sharp tug of beginning climax, and another desperate whimper stuttered from her chest. She squeezed her eyes tightly shut once more, fisted her hands in the pillows beneath her.

Breathing raggedly, Sam forced her eyes open and directed her gaze toward the blond head currently at work between her legs, lapping at her like a greedy kitten with a bowl of cream, and the combination of the vision and that talented mouth catapulted her to blessed instantaneous release.

Though she knew it was coming, she still wasn't prepared. The orgasm caught her completely unaware, broke over her like a high tide, pulled her under as warm tingly shivers radiated from deep in her womb. The small of her back left the pillows and her neck arched to accommodate a long, guttural cry of anguished release. Her breath came in short little puffs and her body shivered and wilted as the last of the tremors tingled through her. A slow, satisfied smile curled her lips and her gaze was inexplicably drawn to Hank.

Male satisfaction clung to his smile and his eyes glowed with smoky arousal. "*Now* you're ready."

Hank stood, shucked his pants and briefs, then fished a condom from beneath a nearby pillow. Sam grinned, recognizing the extra-large glow-in-the-dark prophylactic as one she'd brought along with her. Her gaze lingered on the impressive staff centered between his legs and felt another rush of heat camp in her still-throbbing loins. She bit her lip. Gazing at him, Sam vaguely wondered if the extra-large would accommodate him. Did condoms come in XXL?

Hank's twinkling eyes met hers as he tore into the packet with his teeth. "Wouldn't want any of your stash to go to waste."

That would definitely be a pity, Sam thought, her gaze once more dropping down below his navel. Her breasts tingled and another flame of heat licked in her belly. She was suddenly—inexplicably—hit with the almost overwhelming urge to taste him.

Hank moved to withdraw the condom from the packet, but Sam smoothly took it from his hand. "I'll take care of that," she said, kneeling before him. She set the condom aside. "In a minute." Then she took him in hand, ran her fingers over the hot slippery skin and then eagerly guided him into her mouth.

Hank's breath left him in a startled hiss. "Jesus."

Sam swirled her tongue around the engorged head, immediately fell in love with the way the super soft skin felt against her mouth. Loved the way it tasted. Sinfully wanton…exhilarating. Hank trembled, sending a wicked thrill through her. Her lips curved on a sigh and she scooted forward, desperate to taste even more of him. She framed him with her hands, glided her fingers over him as she worked him back and forth in her mouth. She slid her tongue along the rigid length, under and along the sides, leaving no part neglected. A single pearly tear of desire oozed from the head and she caught it with the tip of her tongue.

Hank had become increasingly agitated during her thorough ministrations, but apparently had finally reached his limit at this singularly erotic act. "Enough," he choked, moving back and out of her reach. "If you keep that up, it'll be over before it starts."

Sam felt a small smile curl her lips and pulled a lazy shrug. "You're the expert." She retrieved the condom, deftly pulled it out of the foil wrap. "Still, I think this will go on better if you're a little…wet." She took the whole of him into her mouth once more, gave him one long, slow suck that made his thighs go rigid.

"Sam," he said warningly.

Sam stifled a chuckle and swiftly sheathed him with the condom. A nanosecond later she was flat on her back, thighs spread and she could feel the hard length of him nudging between her folds. She'd expected him to fill her, had expected him to sink into her posthaste. Instead he rocked back and forth between her nether lips, sliding up and down, bumping that sweet spot at the crest of her sex.

It was an absolutely marvelous sensation, feeling that thick hot part of him gliding between her drenched folds, but as good as it felt, it wasn't quite…enough. Rather than bringing blessed relief to the fire burning inside her, this act seemed to make that achy hollow place deep in her womb expand, intensify.

And from the look of devious delight on Hank's handsome face, she had the distinct impression that he was waiting for her to beg. Waiting for her to tell him exactly what she wanted. Fine. Whatever. She was past caring. She'd waited too long for this moment, too long for this night with him and she'd be damned before she'd be shy about voicing her wants now.

Sam hooked her ankles around his legs and tilted her hips more firmly against his. She rocked against him, almost dragging him into her heat.

He chuckled, the bastard, and drew back. "Not yet," he told her.

And forth…

Not yet? Why the hell not? "I'm ready," she said, her voice an exasperated broken wail. She reached down and grasped the twin muscles of his ass, trying to urge him on.

And back…

"But it'll go in easier if it's a little…wet," he told her, mimicking her earlier taunt.

And forth…

But, gratifyingly, she could tell that it cost him. A muscle flexed in his tight jaw and tension radiated off him in waves. A light dew of sweat slickened his skin. She moved her hands up over his back, over his shoulders and lightly scored his chest with her nails. Clearly he wanted to be inside her just as much—if not more—than she wanted him to be there.

And forth…

Her feminine muscles clenched and her womb squeezed and every cell in her being hungered for another explosion of release. Sam's heart beat wildly in her chest—matched the rhythm of the insistent itchy throb between her legs—and she honestly felt like she would die if he didn't push inside her, if he didn't fill her up. Right now.

And back…

"Hank, please," Sam begged. "Please— Now!"

Hank's tortured yet curiously soft gaze tangled with hers, he found her hands, tenderly laced his fingers through hers, and then with one long slow thrust, buried himself deeply inside her.

For all intents and purposes, the world tilted on its axis, the sky fell and every star in the heavens rained down around them. Little twinkles of light burst behind her lids and her chest tightened, preventing so much as a startled inhalation. If Sam had ever experienced anything so perfect in her life she couldn't recall it. Couldn't imagine anything ever being more magnificent than this moment, than the absolute perfection of their joined bodies. Her eyes misted with emotion and, with as much clarity as can be born in mindlessness, she knew that she'd never be the same.

Hank had unwittingly claimed her heart years ago and she'd just given him her body as well.

Neither, she knew, would ever belong to another man.

13

HANK DUG HIS TOES into the pillow and firmly lodged himself deeply into her hot, tight heat. The relief he felt at finally putting himself between her legs was short-lived, chased away by a sentiment so strong and overpowering that he had to lock every muscle in his body to keep from collapsing under the weight of it.

Something sharp, sweet and, if he were honest, a bit frightening spilled into his chest, making it difficult to breathe. His heart raced and a hot tingling heat swept from one end of his body to the other. He was hit with the simultaneous urge to laugh and weep, and he couldn't for the life of him make any of these foreign emotions make sense. Couldn't break them down and organize them, couldn't do anything at all but hold himself utterly still and absorb them. Wait for the bizarre feeling to pass.

He looked down and his gaze tangled with Sam's. Those pale green eyes glittered with need and something else, something just beyond his understanding. He'd imagined having her like this countless times over the years, had dreamed it too many times to imagine, but nothing could have prepared him for the reality.

Her strawberry curls fanned out on an emerald-green pillow, those sinfully carnal lips swollen from his kisses, her skin flushed pink with desire, her pouty breasts a mere nod of his head away and her tight little body fisting around him in the most intimate of embraces. Just thinking about it made his dick jerk inside her. She gasped, then instinctively tightened around him.

Hank instantly stopped pondering the weird emotions currently swelling in his chest and concentrated on the swelling below his navel.

He slid out of her, then back in, slowly at first because the sensation was too intense not to savor. But then she caught his rhythm and he forgot about savoring, about relishing, about control.

He didn't think at all.

Primal instinct and baser need edged out anything remotely resembling civilized male. He bent his head and fed at her breast, focused on the exquisite draw and drag between their joined bodies, that utterly amazing friction. Harder and harder, faster and faster. Nonsensical sounds broke from her throat, a gasp, a cry, a groan, and he answered each one with another powerful thrust.

Sam thrashed wildly beneath him. "Oh, Hank— I don't know— I can't—"

The fever had caught her as well. Her flushed skin grew damp and she sank her teeth into her bottom lip, clearly on the edge of release. Hank disentangled their hands, grasped her hips and angled her more firmly beneath him. He hammered relentlessly into her. "Oh, yes you can," he told her. "Reach, baby. Reach for it."

He pistoned harder, then harder still. Her mouth opened in a soundless scream and she suddenly arched beneath him. Her muscles spasmed around him, clamped greedily around his throbbing rod. He thrust once, twice, again, then came hard as the climax rocketed through him, blasted from his loins, milking him of strength with each lingering pulse.

Limbs weak and shaking, Hank rolled them onto his side. He smoothed his hand over her hair and kissed her temple. "Oh, Sam," he murmured.

And that was it.

Though he knew there were things that he should say—like, "I'm never letting you go," or "I think I'm in love with you,"—disassembling was completely beyond him. He didn't even have the strength to be alarmed at the L word. Ordinarily, just thinking about love would have instilled a dart of sheer panic into his heart. Curiously, thinking about loving Sam didn't.

It felt right. As necessary as breathing.

But he'd think about it later, Hank decided, as his breathing grew deep and steady and his lids drooped. He'd think about it tomorrow, tell her these things tomorrow…right before he asked her to marry him.

"THINK WE COULD DO IT HERE and not get caught?" Hank asked with a wicked grin. He nuzzled her ear, sending a chorus of goose bumps up her back.

Sam chuckled. Here was an isolated ammunition barrack in old Fort Morgan. Still, regardless of how isolated, there was still the grim possibility that they would get caught. It would undoubtedly be worth it. Remembered heat tingled in her belly and breasts. Nevertheless… "With my luck, we'd definitely get caught."

Hank sighed dramatically. "So that's a no?"

"No." Sam leaned forward and pressed a soft kiss to his cheek, then tugged him toward the exit. "That's a wait till we get home."

Home. Her throat contracted at the Freudian slip, but if Hank noticed anything telling about the remark, he didn't show it, thank God. She really had to get it together, Sam thought as they made their way up to the second level. Honestly, she knew that making love with Hank would intensify her feelings for him—any idiot would have realized that—but she hadn't realized just how much until she'd awoken in his arms this morning and her empty, lonely future lay stretched out before her. Sam swallowed.

It was almost unbearable, but she didn't have any intention of wasting a single minute of the time that she had left with him. She'd have time enough to dwell on her misery once she was back in Aspen. In the meantime, she planned to follow her sex diet—double up on her portions—and spend as much time naked with Hank as she could. She would not allow herself to think beyond tomorrow when she left. Undoubtedly the drive back would provide her with ample thinking time. Winning the SUV had had one disadvantage—it had cut her vacation short. She'd need those days to drive back to Aspen.

When they'd returned to the B&B this morning—after a lengthy shower, lengthy sex and another lengthy shower—Sam had called and canceled her airline ticket, then had phoned work and told them that she wouldn't be in until Wednesday. She'd decided to break the twenty-something-hour drive up over two days. She could probably make it driving straight through, but why hurry? She had no one to go home to, only a job and Cedar Crest could make it another day without her. Besides, they'd have to. As soon as she returned, she was giving notice.

They'd reached the top of the narrow stairs and the gorgeous view of the gulf stretched out before them. Sam moved forward and leaned against the rail, tilted her face and welcomed the kiss of the salty breeze. The afternoon sun hovered just over the horizon, sending rays of gold-streaked light dancing over the turquoise waters. Sam inhaled deeply, let the tangy air permeate her lungs. "'Damn the torpedoes, full speed ahead!'"

Hank nodded, seemingly impressed. "Know your history, do you? See, what I fudged on your Belle form wasn't entirely false."

Sam snorted. "Wrong. I know the history of this fort because I love it. There's something about it that draws me here. History seems to live in the very soil."

Hank nodded, slung an arm over her shoulder.

Built in the unique design of a starfish in the early eighteen hundreds, Fort Morgan sat at the end of a peninsula at the mouth of Mobile Bay. It had become well known during the Civil War when a Union Admiral had lead a fleet close to the bay. During the attack, the *U.S.S. Tecumseh* had struck a mine, and in the confusion, the fleet had hesitated under the attack, at which point the Union Admiral had ordered, "Damn the torpedoes, full speed ahead!"

It was a phrase that she'd heard all of her life, but had never known the history behind the statement until several years ago when she'd toured the museum. Though small, the museum was packed with lots of history. Old guns and uniforms, letters from soldiers who'd been stationed at the fort. Sam sighed. She really loved it here.

A comfortable silence lengthened between them as they both enjoyed the view. For the briefest of moments Sam allowed herself the luxury of believing that when she went off the sex diet that, despite the fact that they'd had wonderfully amazing back-clawing sex, all would return to normal. She'd move back here. They'd still call each other and e-mail, they'd still hang out together and have fun, that everything would be the same as it'd always been. Their friendship would survive and everything would simply go back to normal.

But she knew it wouldn't.

How could it after everything that had happened between them? Last night had simply been… There was no word that could aptly describe how incredibly wonderful last night had been. Granted Hank had the advantage of experience over her, but Sam couldn't help but think that what they'd shared had been truly special. She knew it was to her because… Well, because she loved him. It hadn't been just sex. She'd put her entire heart into the act. And, though it was probably naive thinking on her part, she couldn't help but think that Hank had, too.

Her gaze turned inward, recalled that exact moment when she'd welcomed him into her body.

He'd worn the most curious, equally awed and startled expression. Like he'd felt a special connection as well. He'd locked himself inside her and, for a moment, hadn't moved. Of course, he could have developed a leg cramp. Hell, who knew? Certainly not her.

And in all honesty, it was probably better to believe it was a leg cramp, or some other unknown reason, because daring to suspect that he felt more for her than mere attraction was a danger she'd just as soon avoid. It was detrimental to her peace of mind. For many reasons, the most important of which being her heart. Furthermore, tricking Hank into tipping his hand with this sex diet was bad enough, but tricking his heart as well? That would be truly heinous.

Sam cast a covert look at Hank from beneath her lashes and need and affection broadsided her once more. God, he was gorgeous. He had the most masculine features, high cheekbones, lean cheeks, a strong jaw and a thin blade of a nose…and yet there was something boyish and vulnerable about him, too. Something so sweet that made her heart ache.

He turned and caught her staring and his eyes crinkled as a smile caught the corner of his mouth. He tightened his arm around her shoulders and dragged her closer to his side. "I see a new freckle," he told her. "Did you forget your sunblock?"

Sam chuckled. "A new freckle? How do you know it's a new freckle?"

"Because it wasn't there this morning."

Her lips curled with wry humor. "And you looked at my face close enough this morning to notice a new freckle?" she asked skeptically.

Hank winced. "Not exactly your whole face. Just your mouth."

"What?"

He slid his finger next to her mouth, then followed the path with his lips. "That one," he murmured silkily, "wasn't there. It's new. I know because I stare at your mouth a lot. You have an amazing mouth. Haven't you noticed?"

Sam blinked drunkenly. She'd lost the thread of the conversation. "That I have an amazing mouth?"

He grinned. "No. That I stare at it all the time."

"Oh... No." Her knees wobbled.

He brushed another butterfly kiss across her lips and his voice lowered to a more intimate level. "Your mouth is lush and ripe...very carnal. I look at and think about kissing you...and having you kiss me...in lots of different places."

All of those places flitted rapid-fire through her mind. Then Hank laid siege to her mouth and her mind blanked. Sensation eradicated thought, ceased all cognitive thinking. She twined her arms around his neck, then slid her hands into the silky hair at his nape, angled his head so that she could devour him as well. The kiss was long and hot, slow and deep, and when they finally broke apart, Sam could scarcely catch her breath.

Breathing somewhat hard, Hank rested his forehead against hers. "God, you make me crazy," he growled. "I've wanted you forever, since you got here, since we finished this morning. It's making me insane. We're in a public place, for crying out loud, and all I can think about is how wonderful it would be to bend you over this railing and lift your skirt and... Jesus." He dragged her forward. "Let's go to the car."

Secretly thrilled, Sam allowed herself to be pulled along. "We're going to— In the car?"

He swiftly descended the steps. "It's got tinted glass and good suspension."

Anticipation jimmied a wicked giggle from her throat. Clearly *Operation Orgasm* wasn't over.

HANK CHECKED THE PARKING LOT for other cars and was relieved to see that there was only one at the moment and it was parked closer to the entrance. They'd parked on the far side of the lot, away from the heavy foot traffic. He fished a couple of things from his pocket—a condom and the keys—then swiftly crossed the lot.

It was crazy, utterly crazy, but he couldn't help himself. He'd been a perpetually aroused wreck because of her since…forever and he'd wrongly assumed that having her would at least take the edge off.

It hadn't.

In fact, if anything, he was in a sorrier state now than before. Because now he knew how incredible being with her was. Now he knew how she tasted against his tongue, how her breast felt in his mouth and how utterly wonderful it felt to plunge in and out of her sweet, tight heat. This sort of need was completely out of the realm of his experience and he suspected he knew the reason why—he was in love with her. Hank didn't know when, how or why—didn't care. It was a moot point.

He loved her.

He needed her.

The end.

And he'd have her now.

Hank hit the power door lock with the keyless remote and opened the driver's side back door for Sam. With a scandalous laugh of sheer delight, she hurried into the back seat. Hank followed her in, shut and locked the door. He cranked the power long enough to raise the windows for the required privacy, and vaguely noted that he was glad they'd had the forethought to put them down in the first place, otherwise it would have been too stifling even for great sex.

He felt something hit the back of his head, turned

and with a shock of delight, realized it was Sam's panties. He felt his eyes widen.

Then an evil chuckle rumbled from his chest, he dropped his pants, quickly sheathed himself with a condom and, still laughing, dove at her. She parted instantly—her mouth and her legs—and he plunged into her while he ravaged her mouth with a kiss, sucked at her tongue. Her greedy hands were all over his body, tugging at his shirt, then cool fingers against his back. She skimmed the line of his spine, forcing a shiver that shook him from the inside out.

He took her hard and fast and she begged for more, just as desperate for release as he was. She clamped her feminine muscles around him as he thrust, over and over, until Hank felt the first flash of release stir in his loins. He pumped harder, hooked an arm under the bend of her knee and pushed deeper.

Her breath became sharp and ragged and she writhed beneath him. Her skin dewed and a single strawberry curl clung to her mouth. Back and neck arched, her breasts bounced on her chest as they absorbed the force of his manic thrusts. Then she screamed, her back left the seat in a rigid curve and she convulsed around him, a greedy clench and release that seemed to go on forever. That pushed him over the edge as well. He pumped through the climax, rode the tidal wave of ecstasy until it crested and broke and there was nothing left but a gentle pulsing of contentedness.

After a moment, he heaved himself off her and sat back on his haunches. Her chest rapidly rose and fell and she wore the expression of a woman who had just been thoroughly loved. She flung an arm across her forehead, then looked up at him and laughed. "That," she said meaningfully, "was amazing."

Hank smiled, absently scratched his chest. "I aim to please."

She eyed him up and down and something wicked shifted in her gaze. "I noticed."

"And I intend on pleasing you again and again, starting tonight."

She arched a brow. "Oh?"

Hank glanced at his watch and winced at the time. "Yeah, and we have to go. I've got an errand to run."

She sat up and fished her panties from the floor. "Are you going into town?"

"Yeah." Hank found a napkin, disposed of the condom, then dragged his shorts back up his legs.

"Good, because I'd really like to hit some of the outlet—"

Oh, shit, Hank thought, panicked. "You can't go."

She stilled at his abrupt pronouncement and shot him a look. "O-kay."

Dammit, he was making a mess of things. "You can't go because it'll ruin my surprise."

Her mouth curved. "Another one?"

He nodded. A big one. "It plays in with the romantic evening I have planned."

When he came back from Foley today, he'd have an engagement ring in his pocket. He'd propose tonight. She'd say yes. They would both return to Aspen and he'd help get her packed up and ready to move while she worked out a two-week notice. Then they would return here, get married, have lots of sex, make babies, raise their family and live happily ever after. His parents would be thrilled.

For the first time in his life, he had everything figured out. Hank had never been a man to dawdle after making a decision and the moment he'd realized that he was in love with Samantha, he'd mapped out the rest of their lives. That way, things didn't get complicated. He just had to follow the plan.

Love was not complicated—people were.

Furthermore, he'd begun to suspect that Jamie had been right when he suggested that Sam had been carrying a torch for him for years. He didn't know what had prevented him from seeing it before, but he knew beyond a shadow of a doubt that she loved him as well. Conceited? No—perceptive. He could tell that she loved him, knew it. Telling glances, gentle touches, small smiles. It was all there, written in her face, in her behavior toward him. Just knowing it made an almost painful ache swell beneath his sternum.

Hank couldn't imagine anything better than being loved—and being in love with—Samantha McCafferty, *his* Belle of the Beach. He couldn't wait to share his home with her, to make it theirs, couldn't wait to go to bed with her at night, and wake up with her in the morning. To snuggle on the couch, go on long drives with no immediate destination, to have a live-in friend and lover, partner and confidante.

He couldn't wait to have her.

And, provided things went right tonight—and he couldn't imagine why they wouldn't—his wait would soon be over.

14

SAM TRIED TO FOCUS on something more than the bittersweet goodbye she knew she'd be making tomorrow, but it was just so damned hard. Hank seemed a wee bit tense as well—distracted for want of a better term—and she figured that his mood was simply a result of her own. And she had to stop this, she thought with a silent curse. She couldn't let what she knew was an inevitable end to this relationship ruin her last night with him.

She couldn't.

To that end she'd doubled up on the sex diet portions and antihistamines. While Hank had run his mysterious "errand," she'd hit the oyster bar again. If she ever saw another half shell, she'd undoubtedly puke. In addition, she'd taken so many antihistamines she felt like her scalp was going to crawl right off her head. That was the only good thing about leaving tomorrow—she could go off this infernal diet.

Sam perused the menu and blew out a small sigh. In the meantime, she'd better stick to it, though. "What are you going to have?" she asked Hank.

He frowned thoughtfully. "I think I'm going to have the filet and lobster. What about you?"

Sam had perused the menu and decided that the bouillabaisse would probably be her best bet. It was packed full of various shellfish and seafood. It should definitely shoot her pheromone level up. "The bouillabaisse," she told him. "And I'd love some calamari."

Hank nodded. "Sounds good."

Conversation flowed easily between them, just like it always had. She figured that he'd start in on her moving back here, but curiously he hadn't. Despite whatever happened between them, Sam would move back. This was her home. Even if things ended poorly, she'd rather be close to Hank as not be. So regardless of the outcome, her plans remained the same.

Hank asked her opinion on plans he had for the B&B, seemed particularly interested in her input. They talked about his parents, about the new head football coach at Alabama, her job and whatnot. The usual stuff.

In fact, the only noticeable difference that she could tell was the perpetual look of desire Hank wore and the tender way he held her hand across the table. How she wished it would stay that way, Sam thought with a bittersweet pang of regret. But she knew it wouldn't.

The moment she left, and he was out of range of

her superpheromones, the attraction would wane and he'd wonder what the hell he'd been thinking. She truly regretted that for Hank, but everyone had what-was-I-thinking? moments. He would recover, even if their friendship didn't, and she'd decided the sacrifice was worth the reward. Who knew? Maybe later, they could resume their friendship, though Sam knew it would never the same as it had been before. It would be awkward, but hopefully, at some point, they could work past it. Wishful thinking again, but wishes were all she had left.

"Did I tell you that I found an antique claw foot tub to go in my bathroom?" Hank asked.

Mouth full of calamari, Sam shook her head.

"I'm going to do a massive remodel of that bathroom in the near future. Put in the new tub...and his and her vanities."

"Really?" His and her vanities. Sam felt the bite of clam hit the lump that had inexplicably formed in her throat. So he'd finally started thinking about settling down. Pity it couldn't be with her. "That's nice," she said, for lack of anything better.

"I'd even thought about adding on, but wouldn't dream of it unless I could find an architect who could remain true to the house."

Adding on, too? So not only the idea of settling down had occurred, but also the idea of having a family seemed to have gelled as well. Unless he gave up guest rooms, he'd have no choice but to add on a family wing of the house. Sam was finding it hard to be encouraging, but finally managed to dredge up the required enthusiasm. It was what a friend would do.

"I'm sure that you could find someone who could do the job," she said. "Since it's a B&B as well, it would be excellent advertising for whoever did the work."

Hank nodded, seemingly mulling that over.

Thankfully, before he could tell her any more of his heart-wrenching plans, their food arrived. Sam dove into her bouillabaisse with gusto. The more she thought about Hank and his mythical family, the more she ached. Her chest squeezed and she developed an eye twitch.

"Sam, there's something I wanted to ask you," Hank said, somewhat nervously.

What now? Sam wondered. Did he want her to give an opinion on what he should name his future children? Nevertheless, she pushed a smile into place and looked up at him.

"I'd planned to wait until after dessert, but—" He stopped abruptly and frowned. "What's wrong with your eye?"

"Nothing. It's just a twitch." For some reason, it was hard to talk. Her tongue felt…large.

"No, it's bright red and it's swelling." He leaned forward and peered at her closely. "So's the other one."

That wasn't the only thing that was swelling, Sam realized with ballooning horror—so was her throat.

Rapidly.

Sam tried to suck in a breath but could barely get any air through her tight throat. She gasped and clutched her neck and her frightened eyes met Hank's. Her heart tripped wildly in her chest and her skin seemed to be too small for her body. An itchy heat started at her scalp and worked its way down. She gasped again as her eyes streamed.

"My God, you're having an allergic reaction." His gaze flew to her plate, then back to her face, then realization dawned and in that instant she knew that he'd remembered her allergy. His brows formed an angry baffled line. "You're allergic to seafood. Why in God's name have you been—"

But the rest of what he said was lost on Sam. She clutched her neck and tried to drag in air, but her constricted throat wouldn't let any oxygen into her lungs. Seemingly from far away she saw Hank leap up from the table and grab her. Dimly she heard a series of shouts, the clank of abandoned cutlery. Then she felt a prick on her thigh and, in the midst of all this the words *stupid, reckless,* and *sorry* floated through her mind, then *Am I dying?*

Then nothing…

HOURS LATER SAM DISCOVERED that she hadn't died—merely fainted—but the possibility that she would die from mortification and stupidity was beginning to be a grim fear.

Hank sat in the corner of the Emergency Room on the chair that was reserved for the doctor. "A sex diet?" he asked, his voice quietly ominous.

"Yes," Sam said miserably. Her throat was still swollen, and made her voice hoarse. The prick she'd felt had been an Epi Pen another customer in the restaurant had had in their purse. It had provided enough relief to get her to the hospital, where a frowning doctor came in and generally treated her like she was a complete moron.

Which she was.

What she'd done had been unforgivably stupid.

"Because you wanted to make yourself attractive to the opposite sex. Because you wanted an orgasm." Statements, not questions and his voice literally throbbed with weary pent-up rage. He clearly wanted to throttle her.

"I know it was stupid, but—"

Hank shot up from his seat. "Stupid?" he quietly roared. "*Stupid?* Stupid doesn't begin to cover it, Sam. What you did was *insane!* Crazy!" He speared his hands through his hair. "You could have seriously hurt yourself! Could have died! And for what? *An orgasm?* What in God's name were you thinking? What made you keep eating all that seafood? Why did you go and have oysters at Captain Jack's when you knew we had dinner reservations?'' He shook his head. ''None of this makes sense.''

Sam winced. She'd hoped he'd missed that part about Captain Jack's when she'd spoken to the doctor—she'd had to tell him everything she'd had to eat that day—but obviously he hadn't.

''What? Were you *trying* to hurt yourself?''

''No, of course not.''

''Then why?'' he demanded.

''I've already told you,'' Sam said wearily. She couldn't believe this was the way things would end between them. A lump of emotion formed in her tortured throat and she blinked back tears.

''Then *why?*'' he demanded. ''Tell me why.''

The tears she'd been trying to hold in check finally spilled past her lashes and she gave an ironic laugh. ''You want to know why? Fine. I'll tell you why—you.''

He blinked, seemingly thunderstruck. ''Me?''

''I never expected the diet to work on you, Hank. Never dreamed that it would. And I've wanted you to want me for so long,'' she told him, her voice breaking with an anguished sob. ''For years.'' She shrugged, forced a wobbly smile. Another tear fell unheeded down her cheek. ''And then you did. A-and you made me an offer that I couldn't refuse, because it was everything—*everything*—I'd ever wanted. So I ate more seafood and doubled up on the antihistamines, thinking that if I just kept it up, I could make you want me through the rest of the week. U-until I had to go home.''

"Yeah, well...there's just one flaw with your reasoning.''

"What's that?''

"It wasn't your sex diet, or your pheromones or your new appearance that made me want you—it was *you. Just you.* I told you that. I bared my soul to you, Sam.''

Sam shook her head sadly. "I'm truly sorry. But you won't think that after I'm gone.''

"You're not going anywhere. Do you know what my surprise was for you, Sam?''

She swallowed. "No.''

Hank withdrew a small velvet box and opened the lid. "I'm in love you, dammit. I want you to marry me.''

Absolutely stunned, a choked sob broke from her chest. She couldn't believe it—it was simply too much. Not only did he think that he loved her, but he thought that he wanted to spend the rest of his life with her, too. This was the perfect penalty for her recklessness, Sam thought. The Almighty couldn't have devised anything more crushing, more diabolical. Hank was once again offering her a deal that was too good to be true—everything she wanted.

But this time she had to refuse.

He didn't love her, and he might want to marry her now, but he wouldn't later. He'd see that when the pheromones wore off, then he'd be glad that she'd made this easier for him.

Sam shook her head once more, drew in a bolstering breath and dashed the tears from her face. "You don't love me and you don't want to marry me," she said flatly. "It's just the diet that—"

"*It's not the damned diet!* I told you that I've wanted you for years. Since you were eighteen. It's not the damned diet."

"If that's the case, then why didn't you ever tell me? If you wanted me that badly, why didn't you say anything?"

Hank opened his mouth, but seemed unable to frame a reply.

Sam forced a sad smile. She'd make it easy for him. "Forget about it, Hank. It was the diet, don't you see? You might have been attracted to me, might have wanted me, but it wasn't enough...not until I went on this diet."

"That's bullshit, Sam."

She shook her head, wishing that she could believe it.

Hank snorted, shoved a hand through his hair. "So that's it? You're not moving back? You're going back to Aspen?"

She nodded, ignoring the first part of his question. She would move back, just not right now. "The minute I leave here," she improvised.

"You're making a mistake."

"I've made a lot of them," Sam said wearily.

SHE'D LEFT.

He still didn't believe it. Couldn't believe that she honestly thought that he'd offered her his heart—his name—because of some stupid diet. It was ludicrous. He blew out a breath.

Hank sat on the front porch swing, dropped his head in his hands and sighed. Furthermore, how had his plan gone so far awry? And why had he ever thought this would be easy? Nothing worth having ever was, right? Sam, he should have known, wouldn't be any different.

"So she left?" Jamie plopped down on the swing beside him. Hank had given him the abbreviated version of events.

He nodded. "Yep."

"Any chance she'll come back?"

He rubbed the bridge of his nose. "Maybe," Hank sighed. "But not soon enough. I'll have to go get her."

"That's what I figured. When?"

If it was up to him, he'd go get her right now, but that would never work. She wasn't going to believe his feelings were genuine until she'd had time for that infernal sex diet to wear off. Until her pheromone level dropped. Honestly, he'd never heard of anything more ridiculous in his life. Hank had no idea how long that would take, but figured a couple of weeks should suffice. He shared his theory with Jamie and he agreed.

"It's going to take something over-the-top to convince her."

Hank grinned. He wasn't the least bit worried about that. He knew exactly what to do to convince her.

SAM SHOVED ANOTHER HANDFUL of popcorn into her mouth and absently channel surfed. *Sports—no. News—no. Murder mystery—no. Romantic comedy—yes.* Tom Hanks and Meg Ryan, one of her favorite onscreen couples. The first few days she'd been home, Sam had shied away from anything that remotely resembled romance, but then she realized that this was undoubtedly the only form of love she'd ever be able to enjoy and had decided to embrace her misery. It was inevitable, after all.

She'd filled her fridge and cabinets with comfort food, had rebelled against makeup and hair gel and, though it was killing her, hadn't shaved her legs. She looked awful, but she told herself that she didn't care. If she absently reached for her antifrizz hair serum, she made herself stop. If she longed to apply a little lipstick, she admonished herself and tossed it aside. This was the true her. The natural her. She wasn't conforming anymore.

Besides, between work and wallowing in self-pity, she really didn't have the time or the energy to keep her appearance.

As predicted, Hank hadn't called, hadn't e-mailed her, hadn't tried to contact her in any way. She'd really hoped that he'd prove her wrong on that score, had hoped that their friendship would survive, but she supposed when all was said and done, he was simply too humiliated to contact her. She'd duped him royally with her diet, and she honestly couldn't blame him. Still, it hurt, knowing that the bond of friendship was forever broken. Knowing that he hadn't truly loved her after all, that he hadn't really wanted to marry her.

Sam felt the too-familiar burn of tears and muttered a curse. Enough, Samantha. You were an idiot. When you're dumb, you've got to be tough. Suck it up.

She reached for another handful of popcorn and discovered the bowl was empty. Again. No matter. She'd stockpiled it as well. She got up and had made it halfway across the living room floor when a knock sounded at the door.

She drew up short, frowned. Who on earth? She never got visitors. Probably another lost pizza boy, Sam decided with a beleaguered sigh. Hmm. Pizza sounded good. She was debating the merit of pretending like the driver wasn't lost and snitching the pizza from some hapless soul when she opened the door and found Hank on the other side.

Her immediate reaction was a sharp bolt of joy, which was quickly followed by, *Oh, hell—my hair!*

"Hank?" she asked questioningly. Disbelief and humiliation twisted inside her.

Hank didn't say a word, simply looked her up and down. She was painfully aware of her frumpy appearance. No makeup, no hair gel, old sweats. She looked like shit warmed over. Like her old self. "What are you—"

He hauled her against him and kissed her, effectively ending the rest of that query. He nudged her inside, then kicked the door shut with his foot, all the while never breaking the kiss. He just kept feeding at her mouth, tunneled his fingers into her frizzy hair and molded her so tightly to him that she felt a hard bulge at the front of his jeans.

Another bolt of joy shook her and a flash fire of heat swept her from head to toe. Her womb quickened, warmth seeped into her panties. Her nipples pearled and tingled. Want and need coalesced into a desire so fierce it made her tremble from the inside out.

Hank dragged her shirt over her head and fastened his mouth onto her breast, impatiently shoved her sweats down and out of the way. Oh, God, how she wanted this. She stripped him as well and ten seconds later she was on the floor. She opened for him, desperate for him to fill her, even more desperate to believe what he was showing her—that he loved her, that whether or not she was beautiful to anyone else—to herself even—she was beautiful to him. That it hadn't been that damned diet. That he *had* always wanted her, but more important, *would* always want her.

Hank nudged her channel, then stopped and pinned her with a determined stare. Some tender emotion still lurked there, softening the fierce look. "Have you gone off the diet?"

She nodded.

"So there are no funky pheromones at work here?"

She nodded again.

"And, aside from the fact that I love you, that I've always wanted you, you realize what this means?" He pushed a little deeper into her for emphasis.

A slow smile rolled around her lips. "I think so."

His eyes widened. "You *think,* you don't *know?*" A bead of sweat broke out on his upper lip and his arms were rigid from holding back. She knew it was testing the length of his control and yet some devil made her want to provoke him.

Sam rocked suggestively beneath him. "I'm getting the general idea...but I need a little more convincing."

A sharp burst of laughter erupted from his throat and those sea-blue eyes twinkled with humorous determination. He slid a little farther into her—but, irritatingly, not far enough. "Convincing?"

She nodded.

"Will you come back to Orange Beach with me?"

She nodded and he edge forward a little more...but still not enough.

Hank stilled. "Don't nod—say yes."

Her eyes misted and a short laugh broke from her throat at the reminder. "Yes."

"Will you marry me?"

Impossibly, her entire body warmed even more with delight. She bit her lip. "Yes."

"Thank God," Hank groaned desperately as he thrust fully into her, filling her to the hilt. "Did you miss me?"

Sam's eyes all but rolled back in her head again as another climax rocketed through her. Her toes curled. She arched her neck and let out a long howl of ecstatic approval. *"Oh God, yes!"*

Epilogue

"I'D BE HAPPY TO MAKE THAT reservation for you, Mrs. Allen. When will you be arriving?"

Phone wedged between her shoulder and ear, Hank watched Sam efficiently handle a new reservation and a slow smile rolled around his lips. As he'd imagined, everything about his life—both personal and professional—had improved since he and Sam had finally gotten together. It had taken a lot longer than it should have considering they'd essentially been in love with each other for years, but he didn't dwell on any time wasted and instead liked to think about all the time stretched out before them. They'd married here at the B&B a little over a year ago and there'd been a lot of changes during that time.

He'd remodeled his bathroom, installed those his and her vanities, as well as that old claw foot tub and Jamie's firm was handling the addition for him. He'd promised to stay true to the house, and was using period appropriate pieces when he could find them. Hank winced. He couldn't wait for Jamie to finish up. They could really use the space.

Sam had taken over Tina's job, thank God, and—his gaze slid to the front porch swing, where Tina and his daughter currently sat—Tina had been put to work doing something more suited to her strengths—baby-sitting their Belle. Belle Elizabeth Masterson had been a surprise, but one that had been anticipated and welcomed with whoops of laughter and tears of joy. Hank's chest tightened, staring at her. Big blue eyes and strawberry curls, that slobbery toothless grin. She was absolutely adorable, and quite frankly, though he assumed every proud papa felt this way, he couldn't imagine that a more perfect child had ever graced the planet.

Contentment pushed a sigh from his lips as he felt his wife's arms slide around his waist. She followed his gaze and grinned. "You can quit standing guard. Tina's excellent with her. You know that," she chided.

"I'm not standing guard," Hank argued. Not this time, at least, though admittedly Sam had caught him many times leaning over the crib in the middle of the night just to make sure that his baby was okay. "I'm admiring. There's a difference." He blew out a beleaguered breath. "But, I guess that's a subtlety that's lost on you."

Sam chuckled. "Touché. How about this for subtlety? Belle is occupied, every guest is out at the moment and—" she lowered her voice, pressed her breast against his arm "—and I distinctly recall a certain promise regarding all the orgasms that I could handle.'' She leaned up and licked a path down the side of his neck, forcing a hiss of pleasure from between his teeth. ''I want one *now*,'' she said meaningfully. Her eyes twinkled. ''Say yes.''

A stuttered laugh rumbled from his chest and Hank turned and slanted his lips over hers. Yeah, yep, uh-huh, sure, okay…yes. Definitely, unequivocally, always *yes*.

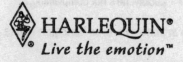

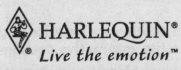

When the spirits are willing...
Anything can happen!

Welcome to the Inn at Maiden Falls, Colorado. Once a
brothel in the 1800s, the inn is now a successful honeymoon
resort. Only, little does anybody guess that all that marital
bliss comes with a little supernatural persuasion....

Don't miss this fantastic new miniseries. Watch for:

#977 SWEET TALKIN' GUY by Colleen Collins
June 2004

#981 CAN'T BUY ME LOVE by Heather MacAllister
July 2004

#985 IT'S IN HIS KISS by Julie Kistler
August 2004

THE SPIRITS
ARE WILLING

Available wherever Harlequin books are sold.

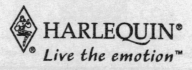

HARLEQUIN®
Live the emotion™

HARLEQUIN® Blaze™
HARLEQUIN® Temptation®

Single in South Beach

Nightlife on the Strip just got a little hotter!

Join author Joanne Rock as she takes you back to Miami Beach and its hottest singles' playground. Club Paradise has staked its claim in the decadent South Beach nightlife and the women in charge are determined to keep the sexy resort on top. So what will they do with the hot men who show up at the club?

GIRL GONE WILD
Harlequin Blaze #135
May 2004

DATE WITH A DIVA
Harlequin Blaze #139
June 2004

HER FINAL FLING
Harlequin Temptation #983
July 2004

Don't miss the continuation of this red-hot series from Joanne Rock!

Look for these books at your favorite retail outlet.